VENGEANCE

Can There Be A Happy Ending?

By

Tracy Ryden

In loving memory of my sister Christine Amanda Strain.

May your memory live on in all who knew you and loved you for being the Brightest Spark there ever was.

CONTENTS

ACKNOWLEDGMENTS

Life. It's unpredictable. It's at times incomprehensible. It's about looking for sources of strength, things to make you find your own peace.

I'd like to acknowledge my dad Andy Strain, whose original idea inspired me to write this book. With an imagination like his, I had to try and make one of the ideas come to life. I found it compelling.

My mum Kathy Strain, who over the years like my dad, has made sacrifices to create a life for us as children growing up, and who is one of the wisest, kindest people I know.

My sons Archie and Chris, may they grow up to believe that anything is possible, and know the importance of believing in yourself, despite anything, and if the odds are stacked against you, to defy and fight harder until you get to where you want to be in life.

My husband Joel, who knows me possibly better than I even know myself, and like my mother-in-law Christine, has been there for my journey in writing this book, encouraging me and supporting me along the way.

My brother Luke Strain, who I love dearly, and is more talented than he realises and gives himself credit for.

My friends Nat R, Nat M, Lady G, Michelle R, Chhaya, Rach W, Asma, Kelly M, Lucy M and Laura, who will all never know just how much I love them and how much they all mean to me.

Rach H (the A-Team!) and my colleagues in Workforce Relations, who work hard every day making a difference to the lives of those who work in the NHS at GSTT.

My aunts, uncles, team photo of 11, plus my 2 cousins on my Dad's side, Michael and Marie, and the Irish Catholic roots which entwine us.

And for my sister Christine Amanda Strain. More talented than I, more potential than I, but never had the chance or opportunity to fulfil her own dreams. Who left a legacy behind her for all who knew her to aspire to do their best, and be their best, and to never let life get the better of them.

Life is about finding your own sense of purpose, own sense of self, and own sense of peace.

Chapter 1

2010. HMP London, England

Nothing is quite as it seems… The predictable, mundane routine of life can be turned upside down in a heartbeat. Before you know it you can find yourself existing in a situation wondering, *How did it all come to this?* John had lost count of the amount of times these thoughts had run through his head as he lay there on the thin, cheap mattress, looking up at the metal slates of the bed above him, wishing he were not there and that he were not so familiar with every detail above him.

*

1987. Majorca, Spain

The laughter of John's children echoed in the

sunshine above the waves of the swimming pool in the September summer heat. Ice creams in hands whilst feet kicked and splashed in the water in the blinding sunshine. John watched his daughters having fun and laughed at their antics. The girls Molly and Kirsty were eight and seven years old, happily enjoying their ice creams whilst his sons were playing volleyball in the water. As they were throwing the ball at each other, Matt was laughing as Oliver missed his aim, landing with a noisy 'splash' which went all over the girls and their ice creams. John's wife Lisa had passed away the year previously having lost her long battle against cancer. John was now the main carer for his children; the boys were eleven and thirteen years old, and they were great kids. With the help of his mother-in-law they had established a routine for the younger children, consistent during the aftermath as possible with what they were used to.

Lisa's mum Elaine came over and gave John a beer. The past year had aged Elaine so quickly and her hair now was almost all grey. Elaine smiled at the children and had been trying her best to enjoy the holiday and to give the children some quality family time. They were the most important people in their lives and it was this resolve that had kept them going.

The summer holiday of 1987 was followed by

annual visits to the same villa, up until Elaine's passing in February 1995.

*

September 20th 1996. London, England

The bar was packed as usual, the dark mahogany of the wood panelling creating a homely atmosphere of warmth and familiarity. To the left-hand side of entering the bar was an old-fashioned fire place, which burned a low heat and added to the homely atmosphere. The lighting behind the bar which shone out from under the high-hanging optics was the main focus of light and because eyes were automatically drawn to this area, there were black boards with bright coloured writing emblazoned on them with the details of cocktails, Happy Hour prices, and upcoming events. The bar had not changed much since the eighties, and Molly who was collecting glasses, wiped her hands on her apron. Ken the bar manager had given her a few hours' work here and there collecting glasses, but not bar work, to see Molly through college as he had been a good friend of her mother's.

"All done, Ken."

"Cheers, Molls."

Molly made her way to the side room on the right-hand side of the bar where the staff's belongings were kept. Molly picked up her college bag and headed for the door.

"See you on Friday, Molls. Take care."

"See you, Ken," she responded, and headed home.

As Molly was leaving a group of the older students from the local university were coming into the bar. "Sorry guys but you've missed last food orders, doubt Ken will let you order anything to eat now, but you can ask," she called over her shoulder as she left. Ryan looked at Molly as she passed them and felt an instant attraction. But before he could say anything the bar door swung shut and the girl was gone.

Molly had started college and was working towards submitting a UCAS form for the local university. The places were limited and the course was expensive. This was when the hunt for a summer job had started. Ken's bar was a local haunt for most of the students and the atmosphere was a friendly, loud, and lively one. Molly had become accustomed to romantic advances and politely rebuked offers with a skill that usually allowed the challenger to leave with their dignity still intact. This usually involved avoiding getting into lengthy conversations with large groups of alpha male types where bravado and humour were the strategic agenda.

Ryan turned back to his pals and Marlon, his old friend from school days, shouted mockingly, "Home-boy's got a crush, man!" The others laughed and tousled Ryan's hair as they made their way over to the bar. Ken looked up from reading the results of the horses as the group of lads came in and nodded with a 'what can I get you?' gesture and the drinks were served.

*

October 20th 1996. London, England

"Molly, can you take a look at the rota for over Christmas for me?" Ken asked casually. It wasn't unusual for Ken to ask this as he would often rely on Molly to be on the ball about shift patterns. Ken was often preoccupied with other things and sometimes wasn't around at all, although Molly never asked him about it, she was just happy to have a bit of extra money coming in. "You know I'd usually do it myself but what with Happy Hour taking off it's likely to be busier than normal at this time of year so I just want to make sure we've got enough staff," Ken continued. Molly smiled to herself.

"Sure Ken, I'll take a look." Molly grabbed the red

clipboard and perused the drafted timetable. "Ken, Lucy's in Scotland for a couple of weeks for Hogmanay, you've got her down for working over Christmas." Molly observed the clash of dates and lifted the clipboard to show him.

"Oh really? You're joking!" Ken came over and took the clipboard. "Oh right," he sighed, scratching his chin thoughtfully, frowning as he flipped the papers on the red clipboard over, thinking about options. "Don't suppose you'd be interested in some shifts behind the bar, would you? I've got some stuff I need to be getting on with," he asked, his mind elsewhere.

Surprised, Molly replied, "Ken I'm only seventeen years old, I don't think that'd be legal." She hesitated and then thought for a moment. In December she would be turning eighteen; if the overtime was good, it could be an opportunity to earn some money towards her university fund. Although getting her dad to agree to her working during the night wouldn't be an easy feat. "What's the pay like for working over the holidays?"

Ken laughed and smiled at her. "Worth your while's the rate…!"

*

It was just after 6.30pm on a Wednesday evening and

Ryan was off to his regular gym session. Ryan's girlfriend Chloe had asked for a lift to her friend's house as usual, which was on Rosendale Avenue, half a mile away but en route to the gym where Ryan regularly worked out. Chloe and Ryan had been seeing each other on and off for just over a year. Ryan had slipped back into the relationship after being out with his mates and drunkenly texting Chloe with the idea of a clumsy drunken rendezvous in his parked car at any available dark car space near where his friend's house was. A consequence of this was Chloe being under the disillusioned impression that their relationship was not only back on but was ready for the next stage. Chloe was impressionable, and seeing a couple of her friends taking this step had made her feel like it was also her time so moving in together and starting a family had become set within her sights. This had also resulted in the couple having their regular arguments about when would be the right time for them to move into together. Chloe was desperate to take their relationship to the next level and sensing Ryan dragging his feet and fed up with his excuses, she was becoming more and more impatient. The result being, the two were repeatedly at loggerheads over what each thought the future would hold.

They were sat in Ryan's beige Austin Allegro outside a block of flats where Chloe's friend lived. Ryan was fobbing Chloe off as usual, and this was not going down well. Chloe slammed the car door shut and stormed off, flicking her long blonde hair behind her. Ryan sighed; Chloe was a beautiful girl who was not without assets, however she was plain, and boring. Ryan, who was in no rush to settle down, was now tiring of her. He removed the handbrake, and sped off to the gym glad that the awkward conversation was finally over.

*

"Molly, I don't want you working behind the bar there." John looked at his daughter with a face full of concern. They were in the kitchen at home; the tiles behind the cooker had been there for what seemed like a lifetime and had been witness to many conversations of this ilk, of a worried protective father over maturing teenage girls. The red and black tiles were looking so dated that they were on the verge of being trendy again as they were now appearing vintage.

"Dad, I already do work there," Molly replied softly.

"Honey, being one side of the bar, collecting a few glasses is a bit different to serving behind the jump during Happy Hour, and I don't want you doing it!"

Kirsty looked up from her college books at the table; Dad was always like this with the girls. Kirsty knew what was coming next and grabbed the opportunity to excuse herself from the conversation which was about to follow.

"Dad, we are not little girls anymore, I'll be eighteen in December! When Oliver worked at that place a few years back, you didn't say a word to him about it being inappropriate."

"That was different…"

Kirsty paused halfway up the stairs and listened to the exchange. It was true, their brother Oliver had worked there before, albeit briefly, so she was curious to see how this conversation would pan out.

"Dad, you can't wrap us up in cotton wool forever. Kirsty and I need lives as well and want to be able to be independent, I want to pay my own way, and besides, I know you can't afford to keep subsidising us."

"That's just it though, Molly, I can afford it."

But she shook her head in response. "No Dad, you can't." Molly had seen a couple of the reminders for bills which were due payment and could not bear her dad being under financial pressure without her helping out.

"I'll find the money, Molly," John replied, being dismissive. "You don't need to be doing bar work, I don't even like you being in there collecting glasses, let alone working there at night when it gets busy, that's when you get all the drunks and trouble makers." John looked worried and the years of looking after children were etched on John's face. He had worked as a site manager in the construction industry for about twenty years and the years of hard work being outdoors in all weathers were visible in the lines on his face. Molly stopped arguing and went over to hug her father.

"Dad, you and Mum have known Ken for years, he'll look out for me, you don't need to worry about me. I'll be fine. It'll probably only be for over the festive period anyway, doubt he can afford to pay me the wages he's offered to pay into the New Year!" Molly said cheerfully with a smile.

Kirsty continued going upstairs thoughtfully. Ken was a nice guy but something about him made Kirsty feel uneasy and although she had never voiced her concerns previously, and nothing untoward had ever happened, she could see why her father was uncomfortable about the situation. Kirsty planned to say nothing until she had evidence as her fears could be unfounded and given that Molly had just made a breakthrough with their dad, gaining them independence, she thought it was best not to rock the boat.

*

Saturday, December 14th 1996

Molly had said she didn't want a fuss for her 18th birthday, but John wasn't having any of it. 'Jerry Maguire' was a film on at the cinema that both his daughters had wanted to see. So while they were out of the house John and his sons Oliver and Matthew were preparing a surprise party for when they got back. Kirsty was aware and was under strict instructions not to be back at the house until after 7pm. As they arrived home, the house was in darkness.

Kirsty took off her jacket. "Here, pass me yours, I'll hang it up," she said to her sister.

"Thanks," Molly replied, passing her coat across.

She walked down the hallway a couple of paces, and pushed open the door on her right to their living room. As she switched on the light, she heard, "Surprise!" and shrieked in response, throwing her hands up to her face, covering her eyes as party poppers went off all around her. There was laughter as Stevie Wonder blared out of the CD player singing, "Happy birthday to you," and people began to sway and dance around. People sang along and John came over to hug his daughter, laughing at her reaction.

"Dad!" Molly yelled with exasperation, smiling happily. "Honestly, what are you like!" Oliver and Matthew came over and both hugged their sister as her cheeks were still recovering from blushing.

Their elderly neighbour Vera stood behind and waited for an opportunity to give Molly her present. When she was able to get Molly's attention she passed over the small parcel, saying, "Happy birthday Molly. It's not much, dear, but you'll be grateful now the weather's getting colder."

Molly unwrapped the gift, it was a pair of beige woollen gloves with a matching hat. She smiled. "Thanks Vera, they're lovely, I'll be sure to use them."

The party lasted until around midnight. John had been taking photos throughout the evening and came over to his daughters with his camera in his hand. "Dad, honestly, you didn't have to do all this. Thank you, what a great party!" Molly smiled as she hugged her dad.

John smiled back. "We couldn't let you turn

eighteen and not have a party, that was never going to happen," he chuckled. "Work's picking up, and I'd already been putting money by for it. The others helped as well so it was fine." John noticed Kirsty was coming over. "Hey listen, you two, I haven't taken a picture of you both together yet," he said, pulling them beside each other, so they stood side by side as the camera flashed. "Say cheese!"

*

December 20th 1996. London, England

Baby D's 'Change Your Heart' was pumping out of the jukebox, the bar was full of festive drinkers in good spirits and Molly was getting confident, learning the ropes behind the bar.

"That's it, Molls, you need to leave enough room for the lemonade, hold the glass to the side as you're pulling the tap, helps less wastage, and pulls a better pint," Ken was saying as he showed Molly around the taps. Ken picked up a beer mat and wiped his hands.

"So these ones are the beer taps, Carlsberg, Fosters and Stella, that one's Guinness and the one over there is London Pride?"

"You got it, girl. Right, your mixers are in there and the bottle opener is automatic on this thing here, your ales are in there and as you know, food orders stop at 19.30pm, no exceptions."

"Right, got it," Molly responded.

"Hi Molls!" Kirsty came into the bar just after 6pm; she had just started 6th form college that September and was on her way back home from the library. Her arms were aching from carrying the books for so long so she perched up on one of the high bar stalls near where Ken and Molly were standing behind the bar. As she pulled herself up and sat down on the bar stool, Kirsty dropped the pile of books on the bar beside her.

"Kirsty, hey, what are you doing here?" Molly said, surprised to see her younger sister come into the bar.

"I missed you and thought I'd come down and see how it's all going!" Kirsty chipped cheerfully. "Hey Ken," Kirsty acknowledged.

"Hey squirt, how's college going?" Ken seemed genuinely interested, and Kirsty was a bit unsure of how to respond.

"Oh, erm, fine, yeah, busy, you know." She looked at the books. "Molls, can I get a Coke when you're ready, sis?" Ken laughed and looked over at Molly, who looked at Ken anxiously.

"Looks like you got your first customer right here.

Don't worry Molls, it's still early yet, as long as you're not buying alcohol you can stay for a while." Kirsty grinned and made herself at home.

The bar was starting to pick up a bit around 7pm. The music on the jukebox was blaring out Guns 'n' Roses' Sweet Child o' Mine' and some students were singing along loudly whilst doing air guitar. A girl from the group was standing up with her arms in the air, throwing her head back as though she were on stage with an invisible microphone in her hand; her friends were laughing and jeering her on. A group of lads at a nearby table were looking around from their booth watching with interest as the group was getting louder.

"Molly I'm making tracks, what time you knock off tonight?"

"Ummm not sure, think Ken said 10.30?"

"I'll come back and pick you up when you're done."

"Ah, you don't have to do that, Kirsty; I said to Dad I'll be fine." Molly finished taking an order and walked over to the taps. As she poured a pint of Guinness, she stopped pouring the dark-coloured liquid a third of the way down inside the glass to allow the head to settle. Molly put the glass down and walked over to Kirsty. "Seriously, you get off home, I'll be fine. It's not that far a walk and there'll be loads of people about as the bar doesn't close till 11pm."

Kirsty shook her head and smiled. Although she was not yet seventeen years' old, Kirsty had her provisional driving license and her Dad John had been giving her lessons for the past six months. Molly had also tried a couple of times, but could never get the hang of it so she decided to let Kirsty have the old red Vauxhall Viva, John had bought for the girls to practice in. Kirsty had not yet taken her driving test, but was well used to the roads so John had on occasions, allowed Kirsty to do a couple of short journeys here and there. "I'll get Dad to let me take the car and I'll pick you up it'll be fine; I'll meet you outside at 10.30pm!" With that Kirsty headed off.

Molly smiled and went back to the pint of Guinness and topped up the rest. She picked up a beer glass, and headed towards the beer pumps. "Was that a lager top to go with that, mate?"

*

Kirsty came back at 10.30pm and waited with the engine running and the headlights on. As she waited outside she flicked through her text messages on her Motorola handset. Ken's bar had been busy that night and the students were taking a while saying their goodbyes to each other on their way out. Molly seemed to have got on well with the regulars and they were waving goodbye to her as they headed out the door. Just after 10.30 an exhausted but jubilant Molly came out and crossed the road to the red Vauxhall Viva. "Thanks Kirsty, you didn't have to do that but I do appreciate it."

"No worries, Molls. Tonight go well?"

"Yeah, actually, really well. Ken's giving me a week's worth of shifts between Christmas and New Year."

"Oh really? You mean you're working Christmas Eve?"

"Yeah I am. Oh shit, sorry, it's Annabel's party! Oh, I'm going to have to give it a miss. Sorry Kirsty." Kirsty was disappointed and it showed, but said nothing and drove the car off the pavement onto the road heading in the direction of home.

"Kirsty, I'm sorry I can't make the party, but you should still go, it'll be fun!" Kirsty still didn't say anything, but instead concentrated on the road. They drove along in an awkward silence; as they approached the traffic lights the traffic slowed to a halt.

"How will you get home after your shift on Christmas Eve?" Kirsty asked, not taking her eyes off the road.

"Oh, I'm sure I'll figure something out. Ken will probably sort a taxi for me or something like that." Kirsty nodded. If she were to say anything now it would appear to be in retaliation to Molly letting her down about the party, but something did not feel right.

"Do you trust Ken?" Kirsty asked.

Molly looked round at her sister, surprised by the question. "Yeah, of course I do, why wouldn't I?" Molly's blue eyes blinked widely.

"Oh, no reason, just a feeling I get sometimes around him, it's probably nothing." Kirsty played down how she felt, but then decided on a different approach. "You know, Molls, maybe Dad's right, working in a bar might not be a good idea, you know what these places are like."

Molly rounded on her sister. "Oh don't even go there, you're sounding as bad as Dad does!"

Kirsty dropped the subject, seeing it was futile. The rest of the journey passed in an uncomfortable silence.

Chapter 2

Christmas Eve arrived; Molly arrived at the bar at 5pm. Ken had put a Christmas wreath with berries on the door which hung heavily as the door swung open. The rosemary and sage scent was delicious as the aroma caught the wind as the door closed. "Hi Ken," Molly called as she removed her woollen gloves and hat and made her way to the cloakroom.

"Hey Molls," Ken replied in between serving the group of lads that had not long arrived.

The Christmas tree in the left corner of the bar was a Noble Fir tree, it had an abundance of blue and silver tinsel with a beautiful star which stood at the top of the tree and caught the light of the fireplace which was on the left as Molly entered the bar. Molly made her way into the cloakroom to the right of the bar and took off her jacket, hanging her belongings on the hooks. Molly came out into the bar and began serving. "What can I get you?"

At around 8.30pm the bar was becoming quite crowded and rowdy. Ken was trying to diffuse an argument that had broken out and was in the process of threatening to bar the ringleader. "Oh come on, mate, leave it out, the guy's a tosser, he was sparring for a fight!" Ryan was appealing to Ken's better judgement and wanted to have the upper hand in the situation.

"Look Ryan, I ain't your mate, I'm the landlord, and if you don't like it, you can sling your hook!" Ken was leaning over the bar and ranting at Ryan.

"Alright, I'll calm down, alright, but only if SHE serves us."

Molly walked over and said, "It's OK Ken, I can handle them. Right guys, what can I get you?"

Ken laughed and said, "OK, it's your funeral," and walked off to serve another punter.

The bar was busy so there wasn't much opportunity for Ryan to chat to Molly as much as he had hoped he would be able to, and this was leaving him feeling frustrated. "Another shot when you're ready,

Landlady!" Ryan shouted out over the crowd.

"Yeah, wait your turn, mate, get in line!" Ryan's pals laughed.

Marlon scoffed. "It's alright love, he'll be happy waiting all day for your number!" Ryan laughed as Molly blushed furiously and continued serving. *I wish they'd just take him home*, Molly thought to herself. As the evening went on, Ken observed Ryan's attentive gazes towards Molly. Molly was busily serving the customers and did not appear to notice Ryan's advances; Ken kept a watchful eye on the potentially romantic situation unfolding in his bar.

"Just one more drink, love, please?" Ryan drunkenly hollered at Molly.

Marlon who was also a bit worse for wear good-naturedly reprimanded his buddy, saying, "Come on home now, man, she ain't interested, and besides she's a bit young for you anyway!" and laughed.

Ryan stood up and called over to Molly, "Come on love, you know you want a piece of the action, why don't you give me your number and I'll take you out sometime?"

Marlon laughed, "Think Chloe might have something to say about that mate!" and threw his arm around his pal and headed to the door.

At 10.45pm Ken decided to call a 'lock-in'. Molly sighed and tried not to show her annoyance. She was exhausted after being on her feet all night and by then just wanted to go home. Beginning to feel she had drawn the short straw, Molly was imagining Kirsty having fun at Annabel's party. Just after 11.00pm Molly decided she had had enough and wanted to call it a night. "Ken, I'm heading off now, my feet are killing me," Molly said, putting away the last of the glasses out of the glass washing machine. She walked over and pulling the hatch up on the bar she turned and said, "Night then!"

Ken looked over and said, "Oh sweetheart, you sure? Was going to ask you to stay back for a late one, there's overtime pay in it for you?"

"No thanks Ken, I'm done in. I'll see you on Boxing Day." Molly went to the ladies and freshened herself up, then headed to the staff cloakroom and fetched her belongings. As she walked out of the bar, the Christmas wreath swung back against the bar door heavily as it closed. Molly walked across the street and put her hat and gloves on. As she began the ten-minute walk home she breathed warm air against her gloved hands and rubbed them together. The night air was cold against her face, shivering, she began to speed up her pace. The evening had worn her out and she couldn't wait to get home.

When Molly got to the street corner she turned right and then crossed the road again. As she did so she became aware of someone else behind her. At first she couldn't be sure if they were following her. Molly quickened her pace and tried to keep calm. She heard the pace of the person behind her had also quickened, into a little jog. Molly's breathing became rapid with fear as she desperately attempted to pick up speed. Suddenly, she felt a hand on her shoulder; she spun around and found herself face to face with the guy from the bar earlier that evening. "Hi there, remember me? We were talking in the bar tonight. I'm Ryan."

Molly relaxed a little but still felt slightly uneasy. "Hi," she responded.

"We're going to a house party, I wanted to speak to you to see if you would come and join us?"

Molly shook her head. "Look, I don't mean to be rude, but it's been a really long night and I need to be getting home. I'll see you in the bar sometime, we can catch up then." Ryan's face fell, he was disappointed the girl had not responded how he had thought she would.

"What, is that you telling me you ain't interested?" He laughed disbelievingly.

"I'm sorry, I just want to get home. Besides, I don't know you and my dad has always warned us not to get into conversations on dark corners with strangers." Molly thought honesty mixed with humour would be able to diffuse the situation she found herself in.

"It's Molly isn't it? Well you know my name and I know yours so technically we ain't strangers." Ryan smiled amusingly. "How about I walk you home for bit?"

Molly felt as though the walls were closing in on her. "Erm, my dad's pretty strict and he won't be happy if he sees you walking with me at this time – but thanks though." She responded politely, and started to walk away quickly. Suddenly Molly heard a loud laugh.

"Ahahahaha, Ryan she told you no! She ain't interested, you must be losing your touch mate!" Marlon drunkenly called out to his friend, as he and several of Ryan's intoxicated friends appeared out of nowhere. Molly turned and continued her journey home. Ryan laughed it off and joined the group of friends at the back. "Come on you guys," Marlon laughed as they began chatting excitedly about the party. At the back of the group, Ryan hung back as they continued walking; a dark look appeared over his face.

As Molly turned into her street, she removed her gloves and began hunting for her door keys in her bag. As she did so she suddenly felt a hand grab her mouth, and an arm grabbed her across her body. Terrified, Molly tried to scream but felt one of her gloves get stuffed into her mouth as she was dragged backwards along the road and down into a side alley. Molly tried to fight against her attacker, scratching their face and reaching for their eyes, as she did so she felt a blow to the head and lost consciousness.

*

Christmas Day, 1996

The police came to the house just after 8.00am. They asked John if Molly had been wearing a blue duffel coat the previous night and what colour her hat was. It was beige. Kirsty stood at the top of the stairs listening to their conversation, feeling her blood run cold. She remembered the hat and gloves their elderly neighbour Vera had bought Molly for her birthday.

Kirsty overheard the police informing her dad that Molly had been murdered. The police said death would have been instant, as a result of the blow to the back of the head. Molly had also been raped after she had died.

*

The hunt for the killer was everywhere, it was on TV, in every newspaper and there was no way of escaping it. The Symmonds family had gone into shock following what had happened and had hardly said a word to each other in the days that followed. It suddenly felt that this was no longer real life and at any time they thought they would be waking up from a bad dream. However, the harrowing reality that followed each waking morning was that this was really happening and that life would never be the same again.

In the days that followed, John could see a change in his sons. The boys, Matt who was now twenty, had become withdrawn. Although he had continued to go to university in the daytime, at every spare minute Matt was either hitting the books in his room or was working extra hours at the local garage Essex Pride, so John hardly saw him. Oliver, was now twenty-three, and although he had always had an issue with alcohol and cannabis, he was now becoming dependant, and was brooding and suspicious of everyone; his on-off relationship with his girlfriend Karen was now over.

Since Molly's body had been found early on Christmas Day morning, by a local dog walker, their world had been turned upside down and there was no escaping that life as they knew it was over.

John had raged that he wanted to see his daughter's body, demanding to know where she had been found. It was like time had stood still, there was no returning to a normal routine in the New Year for the Symmonds household. The police kept a steady presence at the family home, and although Kirsty had been hysterical to begin with, in the days that followed she stared into space unable to remember things, it was like being in the middle of a cloud of confusion. John quickly realised he needed to get a control on his emotions to be strong for his children. He decided to retrace his daughter's steps that night and had vowed to find whoever was responsible for the death of his daughter and make them pay.

Kirsty felt herself being drawn to Ken's bar. It had not been a conscious decision; she just found herself sitting outside the bar, watching and waiting. Just like she had done on the night of Molly's trial shift. She watched as the groups of students walked in and out of the bar, night after night. Some would stop and look at the poster which now hung on the door to the bar where the Christmas wreath had once hung. The poster was appealing for anyone who might have information about what had happened to Molly and anyone who had seen anything suspicious to come forwards. One night, as Ken was locking up the bar after closing time, Kirsty had watched Ken as he was reading the poster whilst locking up. She studied Ken's movements, and searched for answers and any omissions of guilt. Ken's hand touched the poster as he left for the night. Kirsty studied him from a distance; was she seeing someone affected by grief, or was there more to it than that...?

*

January 1997

John had gone into work for a few hours; he could no longer bear the walls inside the house with the memories and had to have a change of scenery. John worked as a Site Manager in the Construction industry, dealing with land developers. This involved meeting clients which he had put off facing. However, eventually John reasoned with himself that if he were at work, then perhaps he could escape the harrowing reality which he now woke up to every day. At around twelve noon John decided to go out and get a coffee and although he had no appetite, something to eat. As he sat at the coffee bar waiting to be served he caught sight of a newspaper article with a photograph of his daughter. Reluctantly, John picked it up and stared at the photo. "I guessed you must be Molly's father when you came in," a woman's voice said, taking his attention away from the article. John looked up to see a waitress behind the counter looking at him sympathetically. "I thought I recognised you from the police bulletins on the TV," she said apprehensively. John put the newspaper down and ordered a coffee and sandwich to go. Suddenly the idea of dining out seemed less appealing.

As John waited for his sandwich the waitress put the lid on his coffee and said, "Not sure whether to say anything but if you're interested, there was a guy in here yesterday. He is one of our regulars – Marlon, his uncle works across the street." The waitress stopped.

John sat back down. "Go on," he said.

"Well, I overheard them talking. Turns out one of Marlon's college pals knew your daughter and had a thing for her. Ryan, Marlon said his name was." John racked his brains trying to see if he could establish a connection with the name to any recent conversations he had had with his daughter, but could not find any. The waitress went back to putting the lunch in a brown paper bag. As she passed it over to John she said, "Marlon was meeting his uncle because he was not sure whether to go to the police about his friend Ryan. He thought Ryan might have had something to do with what happened. I couldn't work out any of the details, but it seems they were in Ken's bar on Christmas Eve."

John's head was spinning. "Really? I haven't heard the girls mention him – thanks," he said as he got out his wallet to pay for his food.

"Don't mention it – and likewise please don't mention this conversation to anyone, I don't want the police coming round asking me questions, my old man ain't exactly a saint. Lunch is on the house." The waitress picked up a tea towel and threw it over her shoulder as the door opened; she went over to help someone in with a pram.

"OK," John replied, "…and thanks again."

*

Matt came down the stairs with a newspaper in his hand. "Do you know where Dad is? I think he needs to see this," he said, showing Oliver the folded newspaper, and pointing at one article in particular.

Oliver took it and stared at it, before slamming down his fist on the table and shouting, "Son of a bitch!" As he got up to leave Matt stopped him.

"Oliver wait, this doesn't mean Ken had something to do with what happened to Molly, but what it does mean is that we need to find out if this is connected."

"What's going on?" asked Kirsty, taking the newspaper from Oliver. "Bar owner questioned over disappearance of teenage girl."

The article was about Molly's murder and also mentioned an old article, dated summer 1990. There was a picture of Ken getting out of a car going into a police station. The article stated: 'Local bar manager Ken Allington was questioned by police today, in connection with the disappearance of seventeen-year-old Heidi Perthwaite. Mr Allington is said to have cooperated fully with the policy investigations and was later released without charge.' The article went on to state that Heidi had disappeared in the summer of 1990 and that she was never seen again. It also stated that Molly was working a shift in Ken's bar the night she was murdered.

"Do you really think he could have had something to do with what happened to Molly?" Matt asked Oliver earnestly.

"I think we need to show Dad and see what he says."

"No, wait," Kirsty said, holding Oliver's arm. "Dad's got enough to contend with at the moment, I think someone should be watching Ken and see what he's been getting up to after the bar closes. Whoever did this may not have acted alone and I want to see who he associates with outside of the bar."

Matt thought carefully, and then shook his head. "Well it's not going to be you, Kirsty, if that's what you're thinking. It's not safe."

"Too late, guys, I've already started keeping a watch on him after closing time. There's a group of older college guys who usually hang around but I'm not sure if they had anything to do with it."

Oliver rounded on Kirsty and grabbed her by the shoulders. "You what?! You mean you've been sneaking out? After everything that's happened you would go and do that, to us – to Dad!?"

"Oliver, I can't just sit back and do nothing, I have to find out who's responsible for this, and I need to do this – please just trust me, I know what I'm doing."

Matt pulled Oliver's arms away from Kirsty and looked into her face. "Kirsty, you know you shouldn't have been sneaking out, it's too dangerous." Matt moved Oliver away and gestured Kirsty to sit down at the table; she relented. "What if something were to happen to you too?" he asked her softly.

"Matt, I'm fine. Look, if you want why don't one of you come with me and help keep watch? It might be our best chance of finding out who did this to Molly."

Matt's face darkened. "No, Kirsty, we need to leave this to the police. I'm going to give this article to Dad and see what he says."

Oliver snatched the article from Matt's hand and shouted, "No! We don't show Dad the article, I think she's right. One of us should go with Kirsty and help keep watch, see what we can find out."

Matt hesitated. "I really don't think that's a good idea, Oliver."

Oliver banged his fist against the table. "Matt, I said no! Kirsty, I'll come with you. We'll see what the bastard's up to and who he's hanging around with. If he had something to do with what happened to Molly, I'm coming after him with you."

Kirsty smiled her appreciation, and nodded. It would have been better if Matt had stepped up, as he was had a cooler temper than Oliver, Kirsty thought. However, Oliver was too headstrong and unpredictable to be argued with. *Anyway; at least I'll have someone with me*, she thought to herself.

Chapter 3

The police had released the body for the funeral and John had finalised plans for the service. As he stood at the foot of his wife's grave, the digger had arrived to prepare the ground for the new burial to take place. John stared at the ground and felt a deep despair rising inside him. All John could see were the memories flashing before his eyes, of his children when they were young, of his wife Lisa, wearing her pink dressing gown, coming down for breakfast, with the sunshine on her hair at the breakfast table. Molly doing her homework with hair in pigtails, Kirsty giving Molly her packed lunchbox which Mum had passed over. "Come on, girls, you'll be late for school," John had said. This was when Lisa had first become unwell, and when cancer was beginning to take a hold of her.

How could I not realise how fragile those times were? John thought to himself. At first, when Lisa had been diagnosed, they were determined everything would be OK, nothing would change and that Lisa would pull through. The denial being so powerful, not allowing for the concept to occur, that it could really do its worst. *Denial is a funny thing,* John thought to himself, *it really doesn't prepare you for reality. Then one day, reality arrives and you have no idea when or how, it's just there.* John crouched down and grabbed handfuls of the dirt, squeezing his hands tightly, to try and stem the flow of the tears and his emotions. He set his jaw into a hard line and stood up. "I'll find who did this, Lisa. I'll find them," he swore to them both.

*

It was late January 1997; the funeral came and went, the wake took place in the house. On the day of the funeral, everywhere Kirsty went there were people. There was no getting away from the looks of sympathy, curiosity, and attempts to ask how she was bearing up. Some people she recognised from growing up, others seemed to know her but she did not recognise them. Politely she smiled and asked if they wanted tea, coffee, or something stronger. The day itself passed in a foggy mist of reality. The police were there, sitting in the corner, watching and discreetly taking notes on their little pocket notepads. Oliver went over and demanded to know what they were doing there, and why they were not out on the beat trying to find Molly's killer. John went over to Oliver and pulled him into a bear hug. Oliver sobbed and fell into his dad's arms. "Son, it's going to be OK, they will find them." He then whispered into his son's ear, "And if they don't WE WILL."

That seemed to be what Oliver needed to hear. After a minute or so he took a deep breath, and rapidly he pulled himself away from his father. "I need some air!" He stormed out. As DI Bates, one of the plain clothes police officers went to go after him, John put his hand against the officer's chest, "Please," he said. "He's my son, please, leave him to me." DI Bates nodded and sat back down beside his superior DCI Sally McColl, as John went after Oliver.

"Hey, you OK?" John closed the patio doors and walked over to Oliver, who was standing outside in the garden, staring out into space.

"No. But I will be if you meant what you said in there," Oliver responded, turning to face his dad. John walked over to his son, casually noticing one of the plain clothes officers had followed him to the patio doors. She was an attractive middle-aged woman, with a stern look on her face as she stood watching the conversation from a distance.

John kept his back to her and motioned with his head towards the end of the garden, and started walking down towards the bench under the tree. Oliver walked beside him, picking up on something. "There's a group of college lads who hang out at the bar. Think one of them had a soft spot for Molly but she turned him down," John told his son as they turned and sat down. "Don't look at me as I say this to you, Oliver, but I think one of them might know what happened."

Oliver stared down at his hands, fighting the urge to make eye contact with his dad. "What do you want to do?"

"Nothing yet." John and Oliver sat down. "I'm seeing what I can find out. There's this lad called Marlon, his uncle owns the hardware store on the high street. A woman in the canteen where I go for lunch told me she recognised me from the newspapers. She said she had overheard Marlon talking to his uncle during lunchtime a few days ago that he was suspicious of one of his mates. Ryan, I think she said his mate's name was."

Oliver thought for a moment, would now be a good time to tell his father Kirsty's suspicions about Ken? Oliver decided against it and to see where this conversation was going. "What can I do to help?"

John looked at his son carefully. "Keep it together, don't say anything to the others and don't draw any attention to yourself because I may need an alibi." Before Oliver could ask for more information his father got up and walked back up to the house; he opened the patio doors, nodded at DCI McColl, then did the same at DI Bates. He walked past a group of mourners that were heading outside with their lighters and cigarette packs in their hands.

*

Matt was standing in the kitchen looking at a photo of the family on holiday in 1987; Elaine must have taken it, as it was a natural shot. The girls were sitting on the edge of the pool, eating ice creams, Dad was drinking a beer in the shade and the boys were in the water playing volleyball. Matt put the photo back on the window sill and walked out into the hallway. "You OK, love?" Their neighbour Vera still spoke to him like he was five years old, even though he was twenty.

Matt nodded and smiled kindly at the elderly lady.

"Do you know where my dad is?" he asked.

"Think he was outside with your brother last time I saw him." Matt went out into the garden but there was just a group of smokers stood there.

*

A few weeks passed. John and Oliver sat in the car, it was just after 6.30pm and they were on Rosendale Avenue. The evenings were still dark in late February so they were parked up on the opposite side of the road a few hundred yards away on the right-hand side of the road, on the hill facing upwards. "How will we know it's him?" Oliver asked his father.

"The guy drives a beige Austin Allegro and has a routine every few nights consisting of dropping the bird off and copping a feel before he goes and plays hard man at the gym," John informed Oliver, as they sat there watching and waiting.

At about 6.45pm a beige Austin Allegro passed them on the left-hand side and pulled into a parking bay outside the flats. From where they were, they could make out the silhouette of a couple inside the car entwining into one. "Dad, what will you do?" Oliver looked at his father.

"In there." John looked at the glove compartment in front of Oliver and said, "Whatever you do don't touch it without those gloves on." Oliver opened the glove compartment and found some black leather gloves. As he went to put them on, his father said; "Now look under your chair, you'll find it. It's got good wrist support so more likely to hit the target." Oliver pulled the heavy dark metal object out from underneath his seat, he held it out below him, and stared at the gun as it glinted in the moonlight, full of promise.

"Let me do it, Dad." Oliver put it back under the seat and looked at his father seriously.

John shook his head. "No, son. This is something I need to do. I've just got to get a few things straight in my head first. When I do you'll need to be my alibi so we need to be going somewhere publicly where I can duck out for an hour or so and come back without it being noticed that I'm gone."

"How about Wednesday when the football's on? There's a pub about fifteen minutes away that gets pretty crowded, nobody would notice you slipping out."

John turned to his son and said, "Yeah, OK. I like it," and grinned with a smile that met his eyes.

*

It was cool March Wednesday evening, a 7.30pm kick-off; John bought a round of drinks at the bar in the

Red Lion and made his way through the crowded pub to where his sons were sitting. Matt picked up his pint and sipped at it. "Dad, I don't know why we had to come here, we could have watched the match indoors. I'm not even in the mood to watch the footy." Oliver picked up his pint, and sipped at it, looking at his brother, and then his father to see his response.

"Because Matt, we have to find a way through this and find some sort of normality, that's why," John sighed.

"Mum would want us to find a way to stick together, and get through this," Oliver chipped in.

"But it's only been a couple of months since Molly, it just doesn't feel right," Matt replied.

"Look, I just needed to get out without everyone staring and giving me the sympathy vote," John said in response to his son. "At least with the match on there's something else other people want to concentrate on."

The match was a feisty battle with neither side wanting to concede a goal. "Oh, this is rubbish!" Matt shouted at the screen, getting into the spirit of the game. "Call it, ref, that was such a foul!" Matt continued to rant, joining in the jeers and shouts of supporters around them.

"I'm going for a slash." John got up and called

back, "Mine's a pint when you're going up next!" With that John was gone, leaving his sons watching the match. Oliver sat facing the screen, but his eyes followed his father's movements to the gents' toilets.

Once inside, John went and stood in front of one of the urinals, unbuttoning his fly waiting for the stalls to vacate. Once the middle stall was free and the toilets were empty, John made his way into the stall, locked the door, gently closed the lid of the toilet and climbed on top of it. As he stood there he felt around the underneath round the back part of the tank. He reached his arm around and found what he was searching for, which he had placed there two days earlier. John pulled the black carrier bag out and pulled out a pair of black leather gloves from his outside left jacket pocket. He put the gloves on, then retrieved the handgun which was inside the bag and attached the sound suppressor.

John put the device into his inside jacket pocket and climbed back down off the toilet, lifting the lid, flushing the chain, and walked out of the gents' toilet. Instead of making his way back over to where his sons were sitting, John walked backwards towards the beer garden which was to his right as he came out of the gents' toilets, checking who was looking in his direction. He was safe as the bar was packed and the punters were busily trying to get the barmaid's attention before the rush at half time. John glanced around his surroundings and quickly made his way out through the gate in the beer garden. As it was dark and the lights in the beer garden focused on the seating area further up, John grabbed the opportunity to duck out of the high wooden gate and around the back of the pub to the car with false plates which he had parked there. John had a contact who he knew through the building trade. They had managed to get hold of some keys for a car lot, under the agreement that their names were never mentioned should there be any fallout. He had parked the car there before the pub had started to get busy, making sure he was not seen. Then he had gone on foot to meet his sons an hour and a half earlier.

With the match livening up the car park was deserted. John jumped into the car and reversed out of the car park and drove slowly, turning onto the high street; he did not put his lights on until he was turning out onto the main road and kept them on a dipped beam for the ten-minute drive to Rosendale Avenue. During the short drive, John pulled a ladies' stocking out of the glove compartment; he grappled with the stocking as the gloves made the job more difficult than planned, however after a minute or so,

John succeeded in parting the stocking, and pulled it over his head.

As he had anticipated, the beige Austin Allegro was parked in its usual spot in the parking bay outside the block of flats. As suspected, there were two individuals entwined in an embrace inside. John parked up on the right-hand side, keeping the engine running, but turning the headlights off. As soon as he saw there were no other moving vehicles on the road, John clambered out of the car, crossed the street, and quickly yanked open the door on the passenger side. As he did so, John leaned in and pulled out the gun, aiming first at the driver, who was leaning over a young girl with her blouse half undone. As the door had opened the young man had looked up at first with a look of annoyance, which then turned to sheer horror as his eyes noticed the gun. Before they could even scream, John fired three times, twice in the direction of the driver and then in the direction of the girl, aiming for her shoulder. John slammed the car door shut, turned and ran back to the car waiting on the other side of the road, with the engine still running. John sped off to the echoing sound of the young girls rasping blood curdling screams of terror.

John drove the car to an underground shopping precinct car park, which overlooked a canal. As he drove into the car park he parked by where the broken street lamps were. Oliver had done his part well. John jumped out, and checking there was nobody around he removed the false plates from the car and threw them both, along with the gun, into the canal. Jogging further down the canal, he quickly cut back down the side street and came round to the back entrance of the Red Lion and made his way back over to where his sons were sitting. The car would be picked up the next day. As he sat down on the bar stool at the table, Oliver made eye contact, and as he did so he said, "This one's in the bag."

John nodded, "Certainly is, son."

*

John had not meant to kill the girlfriend of the young man in the car. The intention had been just to scare her, delay her, keep her afraid enough to not be able to provide the police with enough information to describe the shooter. The intention had been just to injure the girl, and avoid capture. However, the bullet had gone through her shoulder and created an exit wound in her neck, after hitting a major artery, and thirty minutes later, by the time Maxine had come out to see why her cousin and her friend were not coming into the house, both individuals in the car were dead. The couple in the car were Maxine's cousin Sam and his girlfriend Alex. Sam's car was also a beige Austin Allegro.

*

John was watching the news bulletin over breakfast the following morning. He was sitting at breakfast bar in the kitchen, and there was a small portable TV at the end. He had just finished his coffee and was about to get up and leave for work when the reporter on the news turned his attention to the shooting. The names had would not be released until the bodies had been formally identified. Oliver came into the kitchen in his grey dressing gown and stopped to watch the bulletin. Matt was trying to concentrate on his essay about American history for university. He looked up casually and noticed both his father and brother showing interest in the news. "Terrible isn't it?" he muttered, shaking his head and looking back down, continuing with his writing.

"Right, I'm off to work," John said, getting up from the breakfast bar, ignoring the question.

"See you, Dad," Matt said, not looking up.

"See you," John called back.

Oliver went to the fridge and got the milk out, his head still heavy from the previous evening's football match in the pub. "What you up to today then, layabout?" Matt asked his brother, half seriously.

"Oh, this and that, you know," Oliver replied. He had always had trouble holding down a job and recently things had got even worse.

"It is believed that the car belonged to a relative of the family that lived in one of the flats, although speculation over the identities of the victims is still not certain," said the voice of the news reporter.

Oliver looked thoughtful. *If they were relatives, does that mean that Ryan was related to someone in the flats? Thought Dad had said the girl that lived there was his girlfriend...* he thought absentmindedly.

"Oliver you really need to hold down a job, you know things are tight with the old man." Matt's voice pierced his concentration on the news.

"Yeah, yeah, I know, and I will," Oliver responded. "I will…"

*

At lunchtime John popped into the café and ordered a coffee and a bacon bagel. As he sat at the counter, waiting for the waitress to bring his order over to him, the Spice Girls played on the radio in the background. The waitress was humming along to 'Say You'll Be There'. "Order to stay or to go?" she asked without looking up from the till.

"Erm, to go please," John replied. He stood up from the stool at the counter, passed the money, picked up his order and made his way to the door. As he did so, Marlon entered the café and looked around without acknowledging John. Marlon walked up to the counter.

"Doreen, have you seen my uncle today?"

"Sorry, Frank's not been in today, mate, want me to pass on a message if I see him?"

"No, you're alright thanks," Marlon said as he walked out of the café. As he got to the door he bumped into his uncle, Frank. "Hey, there you are, have you seen the news today?"

Frank stopped in his tracks as he was about to enter the café. "Not yet, why?" Frank responded with one hand on the door.

"There was a shooting on Rosendale Avenue last night, wanted to know if you'd heard anything about who was in the car?"

"No, why would I?" Frank looked at his nephew with curiosity; they both stepped outside the café onto the street.

"Frank, the couple in the car were friends of

Ryan's girlfriend."

Frank's face changed. "Stay out of it, son, keep away from that crowd, that Ryan is nothing but trouble and he's going to drag you down with him if you let him."

Marlon didn't respond but took a deep breath and rubbed the back of his head with his hands. Finally after a minute or so Frank broke the silence. "You said the other day that you thought Ryan might have had something to do with that young girl Molly and what happened to her? Well stay away, they might be linked and you don't want to go getting caught up in all that."

Marlon nodded. "I get it, I get what you're saying, but that might just have been a coincidence, I mean, he liked the girl you know." Frank took his hand away from the door and looked at his nephew.

"You mean just like this could be a coincidence? I don't know. I don't like it and if you've got any sense you'll keep your distance, that boy's nothing but trouble."

Changing the subject, Marlon replied, "I've got to go, I'll see you at the shop later." Marlon was due to work later that evening at Frank's hardware store on the high street; he worked a few shifts around his university classes. "I'll see you later." Marlon walked off as Frank said nothing but watched his nephew's back as he walked away.

Inside the café, Doreen was wiping down the tables, and had been casually observing the conversation through the window.

Chapter 4

Friday evening the news came on as Oliver was in the off license buying some beers for the weekend. As he paid for the beers, Oliver picked up the carrier bag and went to leave. As he did so he saw the headlines on the evening's newspaper: 'Couple identified in double shooting as Sam Osbourne and Alexandra Sullivan'. Underneath the headline were two separate photographs of the victims of the shooting, one of Sam and one of Alex. Oliver felt the blood drain from his face, as he started to read the article. "Did you want that, mate?" the man behind the counter asked.

"Erm, yeah, sure, keep the change," Oliver said as he gave the man a pound coin and walked out with the newspaper. Outside the shop, Oliver read the first paragraph of the article and, folding it up, he stuffed it into his carrier bag muttering, "Oh shit…" under his breath.

*

Back at the house, Oliver and John looked at the article in the living room. John put the newspaper down and left the room. As he made his way to the bathroom, a wave of nausea overtook him like a possession; violently he retched, and emptied his stomach in the toilet. John's mind was racing. How had he got it so wrong? The families of these young kids were now going through exactly what his family were going through and it was all his fault. John splashed cold water on his face and buried his face in the hand towel. John stared at himself in the mirror, hardly recognising his own reflection. "What have I done?" he asked himself.

*

Kirsty was getting ready to go out, aware that it was turning into an obsession, but unable to stop herself. She was going to watch Ken's bar again, it made her feel closer to Molly. She came down the stairs and Oliver bumped into her at the bottom of the staircase. "Where are you off to?" Oliver asked casually.

"Where do you think?" Kirsty responded as she

got her jacket on.

Oliver stared after his sister as the penny dropped he called after her, "Wait, you're going again, Kirsty? Then I'm coming with you!"

*

"What do you expect to gain from this?" Oliver said as they were driving to Ken's bar.

"What do you mean?" Kirsty replied with her eyes on the road.

"Look, I think you need to let this go," he sighed. Kirsty said nothing but looked sideways at her brother as she drove.

"You've changed your tune!" she replied. "What's made you change your mind?" Kirsty asked as she noticed the traffic slowing down. She gently pressed on the brake.

Oliver thought for a moment; there was no way he would want to implicate his sister in recent events, he wanted to protect her. Although he understood that Kirsty needed to find out who was responsible for Molly's murder. The question was how to enlighten her, give her the information and closure she needed, without setting off alarm bells relating to the recent shooting. Deciding it was a bit too risky to say anything, he changed his mind and decided to take a different approach. "I think we need to start moving on as a family and start focussing on the future. Kirsty, your birthday's coming up, perhaps we should think about throwing a birthday party."

The lights had changed to red, she put the handbrake on and turned to look at her brother in disbelief. Shaking her head, she said, "A birthday party?! Are you serious? Oliver, do you really think Dad wants to be thinking about going to a party after what's just happened? I can't believe you!" Kirsty was incredulous; what was going on in her brother's head to be so insensitive?

Realising how it must have looked to his sister, he went on, "Well I'm just worried about Dad," he explained. "I think he really needs something positive to think about and to focus on. What do you think, is it a bad idea?"

Kirsty shook her head and released the handbrake as the traffic lights changed to green. She sighed loudly. "Well I don't know, what do you think?" They drove the rest of the way to Ken's bar in silence. As they pulled up on the opposite side of the road, Ryan and Marlon were just coming up the street and were going into the bar.

"Let's go in for a drink," Oliver said, taking off his seatbelt. Not waiting for an answer, Oliver got out of the car.

"Wait – Oliver!" Kirsty called after him, as the car door shut. Kirsty got out of the car and followed Oliver as he crossed the street. As they went into the bar, Oliver made his way to the right-hand side nearest the hatch to the staff's cloakroom.

"Evening Ken," Oliver said as he approached where Ken was leaning on the bar with his pen behind his ear, looking at the horses' betting slip.

"Oliver, how are you doing, son?" Ken replied, putting down his papers.

"You know, same old," Oliver replied. "Can I get a beer and a Coke please Ken?"

"Sure, coming right up." As Ken went off to fetch the drinks, Kirsty rounded on her brother.

"What are you doing?!" she hissed in his face. "This is not exactly what I had in mind, bro, why are we in here?" she demanded.

Oliver looked around to check that nobody was within earshot. To the left of them, round the other side of the bar, at the other end were Ryan, Marlon and a couple of other lads. They were busily chatting to Lucy the pretty young barmaid who Molly had been covering shifts for, who was giggling and basking in their attention. The fire was on low, and the lights were low as usual in the bar, creating dark corners and shadows on the ceiling. "I want to see what they get up to in here. If they were here the night of what happened then maybe one of them saw something, saw someone hanging around, or heard something on their way home."

Kirsty seemed satisfied with his response, but looked worried. "But Oliver, what if one of them had something to do with it?"

Oliver thought for a moment before responding with a smile, "Well then in that case, let's see how they behave when they realise the pressure's on them and that we're watching them."

As he said this, Marlon looked over, and did a double take at Kirsty. Oliver observed and said nothing as Marlon quickly looked away and tried to act casual. He knew, however, that something was not right. Pulling his Motorola handset out of his pocket, Marlon checked his messages and quickly sent a text to Uncle Frank. Ryan was distracted with the pretty young barmaid, when Marlon grabbed his shoulder and said, "Hey, I just realised my uncle needs me to help him with his car, my dad mentioned it earlier but I forgot to go round there. Look, I'll see you later." Ryan waved his pal off, appearing to be far more interested in the barmaid, and had not noticed the change in the atmosphere.

One of the other lads called after Marlon as he was leaving, "You're such a flake!"

"Yeah, yeah, another time, guys!" With that, he was gone.

Oliver went after him, hot on his tail; he caught the door before it swung shut. As he caught up with Marlon outside he called after him, "Leaving so soon?"

Marlon turned around with his hands stuffed in his jacket pockets. "Huh? Sorry, do I know you?"

Oliver walked over to him and smiled. "No, I don't think so. But I think you knew my sister. Her name was Molly." Marlon drew a breath.

"Sorry mate but I don't think so, maybe you've mixed me up with somebody else."

As he went to walk off, Oliver grabbed hold of his jacket. "Molly was working here Christmas Eve, you were in here that night with your mates, weren't you?"

Marlon stopped and made eye contact with Oliver. "Look, you're right, man, we were in here. I was sorry to hear about what happened to your little sister. I told the police all I know."

Oliver looked at him carefully and observed the sweat forming on Marlon's brow, which had nothing to do with the weather. "What about your mates, have they had any visits from the police?" Oliver asked.

Marlon shrugged Oliver's hand off his jacket. "Look, all I know is your sister was fine, she was on her way home, we saw her walking up your road. Someone must have been waiting for her. It's sad about what happened, but I had nothing to do with all that and if you grab hold of me again like that I'm going to take you down. Now fuck off, I got somewhere I need to be."

Oliver stared hard at Marlon as he walked off. He believed that Marlon was not involved, but something told Oliver that Marlon knew more than he was letting on. Why else would he be so defensive? With that, he went back into the bar. Kirsty was finishing her Coke and was about to leave when Oliver came back in. "Well?" Kirsty asked.

"He said he had nothing to do with it and don't know nothing. Let's go home."

Kirsty picked up her jacket and followed Oliver out of the bar. Ken watched as they left and rubbed his chin thoughtfully, thinking to himself. It was a shame what had happened to Molly, but Kirsty was ripe for the picking…

*

When they arrived home, Kirsty took off her jacket off and threw it over the end of the banister, and went stomping upstairs. Frustrated, she threw herself down on the bed, and put her head on her hands. Nothing made any sense. Why was Oliver all of a sudden so calm about everything? What was said between him and that guy outside the bar just now? Her head was swimming with thoughts and she could not calm them down. Feeling as though her head was going to explode, Kirsty sat up. She took her Motorola mobile phone out of her bag and checked through her messages. The last one from Molly just said, "Really sorry I can't make tonight. Have fun at the party x." Kirsty fought back the tears and growled loudly as she threw the phone across the room at her bedroom door. Why had she gone to the party that night without Molly? She felt so angry at herself, and had been searching her mind for answers since Molly had been murdered. Why her? Why did it have to be Molly? The loneliness that had set in since Molly's murder had been suffocating. Every morning Kirsty had woken up, expecting everything to have been just a bad dream, but each day it wasn't, Kirsty felt so lost. At night, the dreams came of when they were younger, making camps in the fields behind their house, summer holidays playing over the adventure playground with childhood friends. The sounds, the smells, the echoes of laughter and excitement, it all seemed so real, only to wake each day and realise it was all years ago and that recent events had happened, were real, and that Molly was gone. Her heart felt as though it were breaking inside her chest, and Kirsty sobbed into her pillow. As the tears came and she choked for breath, Kirsty cried and cried, until eventually, falling sleep, as the tears continued. Her dreams were filled with recent conversations, flashes of Molly's face and echoes of her laughter. It was only recently Kirsty had realised how strange it was that she could have a head full of dreams of laughter, yet still be able to hear the sound of her own sobs during sleep.

When she awoke it was just after 5am on Saturday; she heard the birds tweeting outside the bedroom window, her head was pounding. Kirsty got up and made her way across the landing into the shower. She got in and after twenty minutes was staring at her reflection in the silence of the bathroom. She had wiped some of the condensation away and could see her pale face, with red puffy eyes. "You'll be breaking no hearts today, my girl," she said to herself in the mirror. Kirsty brushed her teeth and put some eye cream on to soothe them. Throwing on jeans and a jumper, she padded down the stairs into the kitchen with her makeup bag and took a couple of paracetamol. As she put the kettle on she pulled the standalone mirror down on the kitchen side and went to work on her makeup. After she finished doing so, she made a cup of tea and some toast. She decided she needed some answers.

*

After she had eaten, Kirsty decided she needed to do something, she wanted some headspace. Oliver was not being straight with her, she could feel it. He had to be challenged, she decided, but she wanted to get some perspective first. Kirsty drove to the cemetery and visited her mother and Molly's graves. The cool fresh air had cleared her head and she was beginning to think more clearly. There were some things which just did not make sense and Oliver knew more than he was letting on. Since what had happened Kirsty was beginning to feel like an outsider to her brothers and her father and was determined to take control of the situation. Ken had arranged the rota swap over Christmas, and although it was never proved he had any involvement at the time, he had also been under suspicion by the police at the time of Heidi Perthwaite's disappearance. She decided to do some digging.

*

John woke up at about 8.30am when he heard the front door close. He got up and went to his sons' bedroom; they were both asleep. As he got to the girls' room he looked in; Kirsty's bed was half made and had the markings of someone who had left in a hurry. He went downstairs to the kitchen and as he went to put the kettle on, felt it was still warm. He reached over the counter on the breakfast bar and picked up the cordless phone. He dialled Kirsty's number, the phone rang out, and he left a message. "Kirsty, where are you? I'm worried, call me back." He replaced the receiver, switched the kettle back on and got a cup out of the cupboard. After he had made a cup of tea, John went out into the garden. The birds were singing and chirruping happily and John looked up at the sky. The morning sun looked beautiful; the horizon was lit up in amber and yellow tones mixed with blue from the sky with the residue of sunrise. It felt at odds with how John felt inside, depressed with the knowledge he was responsible for the shootings. John felt suffocated by the truth and had been considering handing himself in. However, every time the thought crossed his mind, anger took over and boiled up inside him. He was angry. He was hurting. Life could not just carry on as it had been, with his warring emotions. He resigned himself to seeking justice first, then confessing later.

Chapter 5

Kirsty arrived at the library just before it opened at 8.50am. She wanted to research the disappearance of Heidi Perthwaite to see what she could find out. She needed to know the truth because she believed it was the same person who was responsible for Molly's rape and murder. Kirsty may have been too young at the time to understand what had happened when Heidi went missing, but now it felt like a purpose to seek the truth. If Ken was connected Kirsty was determined to find out, and if he was connected, he would pay. Kirsty started going through the archive news files at the library. As she sat there flicking through the screens of old newspaper articles, each time she put dates in around the time of Heidi Perthwaite's disappearance articles kept appearing relating to an old climbing frame which had been burned down. Kirsty stared at the old, grainy, black and white photographs; there were pictures from before the climbing frame had been burned down with children playing on the slide, and pictures of the aftermath. All that was left of where the climbing frame once stood was a burned patch of grass with some smouldered foundations of what had once stood so huge and dominating in the middle of an oasis point surrounded by trees.

Kirsty had vague memories of the wooden climbing frame. She could recall the arrival of it one day in the park when she was around seven years old. It had only been there a few years before vandals had burned it down one Sunday night, leaving a burned-out shell of remains. At the time it had been so disappointing to arrive at the park one day only to find the climbing frame had gone. Nobody knew exactly what had happened to it but rumours were that some teenagers involved in drugs had torched it over the weekend. Kirsty flicked through more articles until she found one relating to Heidi. There was a picture of a group of teenagers and Heidi was wearing jeans, trainers and a jumper and was laughing with a group of friends leaning on an old red Volkswagen car. She was pretty, with fair hair and a cheerful demeanour. Kirsty scrolled across again, in the next picture was Heidi a couple of years younger in her school uniform. Again the photograph was black and white, but Kirsty could make out the fair hair and blue eyes that stared back at her innocently. Kirsty shivered involuntarily. She scrolled across again, and there were more pictures. This time there was an article which alluded to the climbing frame being linked to Heidi's disappearance. Kirsty gasped; she had thought she had heard all the rumours which were going around at the time, although this one was new to her.

'Heidi's Last Known Sighting?' read the headline, below which was a picture of the climbing frame. 'One Sunday evening in the summer, after being down the park with friends this was the last known sighting the police recorded of teenager Heidi Perthwaite.' The article went on to state that Heidi had been drinking alcohol with her friends that evening and that some of the group had gone home earlier, leaving a few behind in the park, Heidi being one of them. The police had found some empty burned cans of K and Diamond White the next day upon arrival at the scene. One of the local residents had been walking their dog and came across the burned climbing frame, and had reported it to the police. It was not until later that the teenager was reported missing as her parents had thought Heidi had been staying over at her friend's house, so the alarm was not raised until around 4pm on Monday afternoon. The friend of Heidi's whose house she was supposed to be staying at, had been covering for her as Heidi had wanted to spend Sunday night with her boyfriend. The boyfriend her parents apparently knew nothing about. Kirsty continued scrolling through the articles. 'Heidi's Boyfriend Was Cheating', announced the next headline. There was another black and white photograph, of a young man, around seventeen years of age, looking sheepishly at the camera, walking with his hands in his pocket.

It transpired Heidi had found out that evening he was being unfaithful and had stormed off after a row. That was the last time Heidi was seen alive. Kieran, Heidi's boyfriend, had been seeing another girl behind Heidi's back, someone from the same group of friends; they had stayed at the park after Heidi had left on her own. One of the last sightings of Heidi had been by one of the group's circle of friends called Joe Allington, he was with the group in the park that night. Kirsty gasped. "Allington!" she exclaimed. *He must be a relation of Ken's*, she thought to herself. It was funny she did not ever recall Ken mentioning he had a son. Kirsty printed the article and went back to searching again. She scrolled forwards then backwards as something caught her attention. 'Bar Owner Questioned Over disappearance of Teenage Girl' was the next heading she stopped at. It was the same article that Matt had come across. As she skimmed the article it soon became clear that Joe Allington was Ken's nephew who had been staying with him for a while. Ken had been released without charge as there was no evidence he had any connection to Heidi or that he had ever met the teenage girl, despite Joe making friends with Heidi during his stay at his uncle's house. Kirsty printed the article and went over to the counter. "Can I get two printouts on A4 please?" she asked the woman behind the library desk. "How much is that?"

"That'll be twenty pence please, love."

"Thank you," she said as she handed over the money and walked out of the library.

*

Kirsty made her way into the local police station on Carter Street. It was an old building with huge steps outside. The desk sergeant looked up from his notes. "Yes love, can I help you?" the police officer asked politely. Kirsty got her breath back and showed the officer the articles.

"I hope so, Officer, I'd like to find out whether there was ever any follow-up to Ken Allington's link to Heidi Perthwaite's disappearance."

The police officer looked surprised, and took the articles from her, glancing down at them. "Can I ask why it is that you want to know this, young lady?" he responded.

Kirsty felt patronised and it showed. Taking a deep breath as she attempted to steady her nerves, she made eye contact with the officer and replied calmly, "Because I am Molly Symmonds' sister and I think he could have had something to do with what happened to her," she declared.

The desk sergeant called over his shoulder, keeping his eyes on Kirsty, "Bates, tell McColl there's someone here to see her." Then to Kirsty he said, 'Take a seat, love, she'll be out in a moment. Can I take your name?"

Walking back to the row of chairs facing the desk, she replied, "Kirsty Symmonds."

After around fifteen minutes a middle-aged woman wearing a dark suit with a white shirt came to the desk. "Kirsty Symmonds?"

"Yes, that's me," Kirsty replied, rising out of her seat, suddenly anxious whether she was doing the right thing.

DCI Sally McColl looked the nervous teenage girl up and down, estimating her correctly to be around seventeen years of age. "I'm DCI Sally McColl. Do you want to come through?" the older woman asked as she held open the door.

As she approached the door to follow the DCI, she hesitated in at the doorway. DCI McColl felt a pang of sympathy for the teenage girl. "It's OK love, whatever you want to talk to me about will be completely confidential." Kirsty smiled at the reassurance and followed DCI Sally McColl through the door and into a corridor. As they walked along the corridor they passed several rooms with their doors closed. The older woman stopped outside a room to their right and opened a door. Sliding a green 'Vacant' sign to reveal a red 'Occupied' sign, she waited until Kirsty had entered the room then closed the door. Inside the room was a small round coffee table, surrounded by a selection of soft single green chairs. The room had green blinds on the windows, which matched the chairs. The midday sun shone brightly through the window over the seats. Shielding her eyes, DCI Sally McColl walked over and partially closed the blinds on one of the windows. "That's better, please, take a seat." She waved at the chairs.

Kirsty took a seat, and the police woman took a seat on the opposite side of the small, round, pinewood coffee table. "Thank you." Polite Kirsty smiled nervously at the officer.

"So would you like to tell me why you're here?"

Kirsty took a deep breath and made a start. "I went to the library today; I was reading up on Heidi Perthwaite…" Her voice trailed off.

"The girl who disappeared a few years ago?" The police officer finished the sentence for her. "Yes, I remember the case, it was one of my first when I started here," the officer said rubbing her chin thoughtfully. "Do you have some new information for us?"

Kirsty hesitated nervously, and then nodded her head in response. "I think it's connected to what happened to my sister Molly. I know it sounds crazy but I believe Ken Allington is connected to them both." Kirsty looked pleadingly at the DCI. "I saw the way he was with her, my sister I mean. I know she didn't understand what I was fussing about but I've never trusted him and what happened to Molly occurred after her first shift working behind Ken's bar." Kirsty paused. She could tell how this was sounding and knew she appeared to be reaching.

"Before she started working behind the bar that night, Molly had been earning a bit of extra money, just collecting glasses and stuff; she was saving towards her university fund. Molly was going to be a doctor; she spent her whole life working towards it. Ken gave Molly a few hours here and there to help her save, you know?" Kirsty looked at the DCI.

"It sounds like he was trying to help your sister Molly," DCI McColl responded.

Kirsty became agitated, pulled a face and gasped, losing patience. "No, that's what he wanted her to think!"

"But you don't believe that? You think he was doing it for some other reason?" DCI McColl asked.

"Well, yes," Kirsty said honestly. "I think he was after her, I saw the way he used to look at her." The DCI shook her head. Although she admired Kirsty's brave approach, there was no evidence to support Kirsty's claims other than the teenage girl's words, and it was hearsay. Before she could respond Kirsty continued, "I've read about the new National DNA Database." She paused.

"Yes, this was set up last year," DCI McColl responded quizzically.

"Was there ever any evidence stored from the climbing frame which was burned down in Dickens Garden's park the same night Heidi disappeared?"

DCI McColl looked surprised; the teenager had obviously been doing some research. "Well yes, there was, but not much," she replied, thinking of the burned cans of K and Diamond White which had been retrieved from the scene and had been kept somewhere in the storage vault. "But we would need something to go on to take another look at the case. As you can probably imagine there are lots of other investigations going on with substantial leads that are currently being followed up. For the Heidi Perthwaite case to be reopened there would need to be new reason to have another look at the case," the DCI responded, sitting forwards, clasping her hands together thoughtfully.

"OK," Kirsty replied, sitting back, "what do you need? I'll get you something, whatever it takes."

DCI McColl waved one hand in the air, amused but serious. "Now don't you go making a nuisance of yourself, otherwise you'll be here under very different circumstances," she warned.

"I won't," Kirsty replied, sitting up straight. "I promise I won't."

Chapter 6

It was early April in 1997. Ryan washed his face in the bathroom mirror. He lathered up some shaving foam, and smoothed it all over his jaw and neck. Picking up his razor he carefully, expertly began shaving his jaw with his new razor. His mum always did have good taste when it came to buying the best of appliances. Ryan shaved one side of his face then wiped the excess foam away with the dark grey towel he had wrapped around his shoulders. Moving onto the other side of his face, Ryan rinsed the razor in the sink of tepid water below him. Finishing his neck and jawline, he wiped the excess foam away, rinsed his face with clean running water, and pulled the plug out of the sink. Throwing the towel into the linen basket, he picked up a new one from the bathroom shelf and began rubbing his face dry. He vainly stared at his reflection in the bathroom mirror which had begun to steam up. Muttering his annoyance, he wiped away the condensation then scrutinised his face for any missed shaving patches. He smiled approvingly at his reflection. His mind began to wander and he started thinking about the girl from the bar, Molly. At the memory of her face and the way she had looked at him, the terror in her eyes, he pushed the thought from his mind and tried to ignore the feelings of guilt that were beginning to creep up on him at regular intervals. *Why should I feel guilty? It was an accident,* he thought to himself. *The stupid bitch was asking for it.* Rationalising, how was he to know she would knock him back, and in front of his friends. At this sense of injustice, he sighed and let go of any feelings of guilt, reasoning with himself that she had got what was coming to her.

Ryan was not used to being turned down, and having been new to the experience of not getting his own way with a girl, he did not look kindly on Molly's attempt to 'play it cool' which was how he saw Molly had been behaving towards him. It just seemed unfathomable to him that a girl would not find him attractive or want to get to know him. From a young age, Ryan had been used to being smothered with affection from girls; he was always the Romeo amongst the ladies.

Turning his attention to selecting his aftershave, he poured some into his hands and patted his face and neck with it, hissing at the sting as the liquid hit some broken skin. As he walked out of the bathroom, he began humming to himself and walked into his bedroom, and over to the large white wardrobe. Selecting a crisp, short-sleeved white shirt, he pulled it off the hanger and put it on. He loved the smell of the fresh starch his mother used and smiled to himself as he buttoned up his shirt. Pulling on some jeans and grabbing his trainers, he strolled downstairs. As he did so, the doorbell went.

Ryan walked over and opened the front door, leaning out as he fixed his collar on his shirt. "Oh hey dude, what's happening, man?" he said as he saw Marlon standing looking slightly uncomfortable on his doorstep with his hands stuffed in his jacket pockets.

"Hey man, oh nothing much, just thought I'd come see if you're out later tonight."

"Why, where are you off to?" Ryan asked, opening the door so his friend could follow him into the house.

"Oh, not sure yet, was thinking of Ken's bar," Marlon replied as he followed him through to the kitchen.

"I've got a lecture this morning, starts in about forty-five minutes so I'm going to the campus for that," Ryan said, thinking of the pretty brunette that sat near the front row who had caught his eye.

"OK, well what about later? Want me to come by for you about six?" Marlon asked, psyching himself up to ask what he had been putting off.

"Yeah sure, want a Coke?" Ryan asked, grabbing a can out of the fridge.

"Sure, thanks mate," Marlon replied. "Hey, the cops have been around asking questions about that girl Molly that was killed, have they been to see you guys?" Marlon asked.

Ryan paused for a moment, appearing to ponder on the question, then after a moment or so he responded, "...Erm, yeah, sure, they did a while back just after it first happened. Told them what I know and haven't heard from them since. Why do you ask?" Ryan walked over with two cans of Coke and handed one to Marlon. He opened the can and took a swig.

"Just wondered, that's all. You might have been the last person alive to see her, just wondered if you recalled anything." Marlon opened his can and also took a sip, grateful for the dry hoarseness of his throat abating as he gulped down the cool acidic liquid. It was cold on the back of his throat and made him shiver as he swallowed.

Ryan didn't say anything but took another swig of his can of coke. He put the can down on the counter and slowly walked across to the pile of papers at the end of the breakfast bar. He shuffled them idly, picking them up, he walked back over and put them in his rucksack, which was also on the counter. After a few seconds he replied; "Oh I don't know, man, memories pretty hazy, you know how it is. We had a lot to drink that night and I'd had a few lines, we all did, it was Christmas Eve after all!" Ryan laughed casually, "I told the coppers that she'd said she'd call me and we were going to meet up, it never happened though, for obvious reasons. Shame, I liked that girl, we could've had something" Ryan appeared sad at the reflection of this. "I told the coppers I went to the party with you guys, we were all together when she walked off. Remember?"

Marlon listened to the explanation Ryan gave, but didn't respond to the question. Something did not ring true, so he probed further. "Ryan, you didn't get there till a while after us, we left the bar at around 11pm, I didn't say anything to the police about it but Ryan, what happened after we left you talking to Molly?"

Ryan stopped and looked at his friend, shocked. "What the hell are you trying to say Marlon?" Ryan demanded, a dark shadow crossing his face as his temper began to rise, "She knocked me back, if you remember, so I came with you guys. We went to the party together, I was there with you!" he replied furiously. "Are you implying something? Because while you were chatting football or whatever it was, I was with Mark Turner in the kitchen, so I suggest you watch what you're saying!" Ryan shouted at Marlon.

Marlon felt uncomfortable and it showed; but he couldn't be sure Ryan was with them as they had all walked off, he had been distracted by the conversation about the party at the time, Marlon reasoned that Ryan must have been with them and started to feel guilty; "OK, OK Ryan, calm down, I was only asking!" he said.

Marlon had also had quite a bit to drink that night, as well as a line of cocaine. He recalled the conversation about football, but not much else; other than being plied with drink and taking part in a drinking game which had become quite competitive that night. "Listen Ryan, I'm sorry, I didn't mean anything by it. Look, I've got to go, I'll come by for you around six yeah?"

As Marlon left the house his mind began to wander. *It couldn't have been Ryan, he wouldn't have, he couldn't have...* he mused to himself. *Mark would have said something by now.* Satisfied that Ryan had nothing to do with Molly's murder, he stuffed his hands into his jacket pockets, and strolled off to work at his uncle's store.

Chapter 7

It was late April, John and Oliver were in the kitchen at home. Oliver was reading a newspaper at the breakfast counter, whilst John was turning the washing machine on. They both turned as they heard the front door go and made eye contact with each other. Kirsty came in and put down her bag on the counter. "Where have you been?" John asked his daughter, irritated. "I've been trying to get hold of you, try turning your phone on."

Kirsty sighed, "I was driving, Dad, so I couldn't answer." John stared at his daughter, waiting for an answer. "I've been to the library," she replied, getting herself a drink. "I'm going out again in a bit, I want to go and see a friend," Kirsty said.

"Which friend?" Oliver asked curiously.

"Just a friend, Oliver, why do you want to know?"

"Just asking. Why, are you hiding something?"

"Oh Oliver, give it a rest would you?" Kirsty stormed out of the kitchen and went upstairs to her room.

John turned to Oliver. "Do you think she knows something?" he asked his son.

Oliver shook his head. "No, don't think so, how would she?" he replied.

*

Kirsty sat down on her bed and spread the newspaper clippings in front of her. As she looked through the articles, one mentioned a housing estate about a mile away that Kirsty was familiar with. 'Neckinger Estate Teenage Girl Goes Missing,' stated one article. Kirsty knew the estate and decided she would go over there to see what she could find out. *Where do I start though?* she thought to herself. As Kirsty thought about this, she looked through the articles and lay down on her bed. She fought back tears of frustration, though however hard she tried, the tears came. Eventually, she fell into an exhausted, deep, dreamless sleep.

When she awoke, most of the day had gone. Kirsty

made her way downstairs and went to the sink to get a glass of water. Realising she hadn't eaten all day, she put some bread in the toaster. Whilst Kirsty had been sleeping, Oliver had gone out to the pub to watch football and John had joined him. Matthew, who was in his room, came downstairs. "Oh, hi Kirsty," Matthew said, coming into the kitchen. "I didn't realise anybody was home."

"Hi Matt," she replied, "I've been asleep." She half smiled. "Want a cuppa?"

"Yeah, go on then," he replied, joining her on one of the seats at the breakfast counter. "You OK?" Matt asked with concern. "I haven't seen much of you these last few days."

"Yeah, I'm fine, I just needed to get my head straight about a few things." Kirsty got up and made the tea and buttered her toast, putting more bread in the toaster for Matthew.

"You know if you want to talk…"

"No, I'm fine," she cut him off, not wanting to be interrogated or feeling up to talking. Kirsty also knew if her brother had any idea of what she was thinking he would only try to discourage her and talk her out of it. "What have you been up to today anyway?" she asked, changing the subject as she passed her brother his tea.

"I've got an assignment due in on Monday morning so I've been working on, the 'Greatest Leaders in American History'," he chuckled. "Did you know Abraham Lincoln had striking similarities to JFK?"

"No, really? How so?" Kirsty asked as she tucked into her toast.

"Well, both leaders were elected to the House of Representatives in '46, both were losing candidates for their party's vice-presidential nominations in '56," Matt replied, going over to fetch the toast which had just popped up. As he began buttering he said, "Also, both were concerned with issues affecting African Americans and were active with their similar views in '63. The most craziest thing of all is they were both shot in the head whilst seated beside their wives, on a Friday. There's also some other stuff about the location of their assassinations, fascinating stuff."

Kirsty listened with interest and as she cocked her head to one side she stared at Matthew in admiration.

"What?" he asked self-consciously.

"How do you do it, Matt?"

He looked at his sister, confused, "Do what? You've lost me."

Kirsty sighed. "I don't know, carry on like you do, get up every day, carry on with your studies and continue with life like you do? How can you manage to concentrate on your assignments? I can barely get through each day," she said sadly. Kirsty had stopped going to some of her classes, and even the ones that she did go to, her head wasn't there.

Matthew smiled but looked sad. He shook his head and just said, "I don't know really, I just do." He ate his toast quietly, then after a couple of minutes he took a sip of his tea. "I just think it's what Molly would have wanted. When I think about all her potential and remember how excited she was to be going to uni, it's something she was working her whole life towards... she would have been a great doctor, Kirsty, she cared about others. Molly was a hard worker and her studies were really important to her, I want to carry on that legacy I suppose, I feel I have to. I have to finish my course and make something of myself otherwise what's the point of it all? Molly would have no legacy and what happened to her will be taking away so much more than it already has taken from our family already. I can't let that happen." Matt's eyes filled with tears as his voice trailed off. He stared at the counter. He brushed the tears away with a brisk hand movement.

Kirsty looked at her brother and suddenly realised how much alike Matt and Molly were. She could understand Matt's sense of responsibility and wanting to carry on and make something of himself, to make Molly proud. Kirsty went over to Matthew and hugged him to her tightly. "Molly would be so proud of you, Matt," she said.

Matthew hugged her back and then pulled away and said, "I've got to go, I need to get back to my studies."

"Sure, OK, I understand. I'm off out in a bit anyway, will be back in a couple of hours. Fancy a drink at Ken's bar tonight?"

Matt looked at her hesitantly, then said, "Sure, why not? I can get there about 8 o'clock."

"Perfect, see you then." She smiled back.

*

After Kirsty had finished her tea and toast, she went upstairs, showered and changed. It was early evening, so she threw on a pink shirt and pair of jeans and boots. She sat in front of her dressing table and picked up a photo of her and Molly which was taken at Molly's 18th birthday party in December. Thinking about what Matt had been saying, she decided maybe Oliver was right, maybe she should think about having a party for her birthday. She decided to discuss it with Matt later on that evening, maybe he would help arrange getting some friends together, for a few drinks. Molly wouldn't want her to not celebrate her birthday, and she realised that she had to find a way to carry on like Matt had. As she did her makeup in the mirror, she finished up and caught sight of the newspaper clippings that were in a pile on the floor in the reflection behind her. She turned around, went over and picked them up. Picking up her bag, she put them in her satchel and went downstairs, picked up her jacket, grabbed her keys and left the house.

Kirsty drove over to Neckinger Estate. She had seen a picture of Heidi's house on one of the articles from the library; the house had a hanging plant pot outside with a wind chime in the background. Kirsty drove around the block and as she turned right into the central square she recognised the house immediately from the newspaper clippings. Kirsty slowed the car down as she drove past, and found somewhere to park. Switching off the engine, she got out and walked over to the house, putting her satchel strap over her head and pulling her bag to one side. She coughed nervously as she walked over to the front door, and rang the doorbell. An excitable dog barked, it sounded like a small dog that had a lot of energy as it bounded up to the inside of the front door, getting under the feet of someone in the process, who was making their way to answer the door. "Herbie, no, get out of the way. OK, OK, let me answer it then!" a woman's voice said as the door opened.

Kirsty took a breath as she found herself face to face with Heidi's mother. The resemblance was astounding. The years were there, but she could see the likeness between mother and daughter.

"Yes, can I help you?" the woman asked. She was around fifty years old, still a good-looking woman, with blonde greying hair and piercing blue eyes. She had a black top and brown jeans on. She bent down and picked up the Yorkshire terrier, waiting for Kirsty to answer.

"Hi, my name is Kirsty Symmonds, I was wondering if I could talk to you about your daughter Heidi?"

The woman froze, and looked at Kirsty with wide eyes of uncertainty. "I wouldn't take up much of your time, I just wanted to ask you a few questions – I'm not a reporter – or a police officer – I'm… I'm…"

The woman sighed and responded, "I think I know who you are. You're Molly's sister, aren't you?"

Kirsty was shocked and her jaw dropped as she stammered, "Yes, yes that's right, but how do you know…?"

"How do I know who you are? I recognise you from the newspapers." Kirsty was on the back foot and didn't quite know what to say. "It's alright, you can come in." Jodie Perthwaite opened the door wider and stepped to one side. "The living room is up there on the right, come in."

Kirsty made her way into the house and followed Jodie's instructions. As she entered the living room, she stared at all the photos of Heidi that decorated the walls. She walked over and started looking at each of them. "Are there any new leads?" she asked Jodie as she came into the living room.

Jodie shook her head as she put the dog down. "No," she replied hopelessly. "You'd think after all this time I wouldn't still expect it to be Heidi when the door goes," she said sadly. "So what did you want to know?" Kirsty sat down on the cream sofa beside Jodie and took a note pad and pen out of her satchel. "I thought you said you wasn't a reporter?" she laughed.

Kirsty laughed nervously. "I'm not, I'm really not, I just want to take down few notes and not miss anything." Kirsty focussed her attention on her note pad and asked, "So Heidi had a boyfriend at the time."

"Yes, that's right, Kieran Kennedy. He was a couple of years older than her, probably the reason she didn't tell us about him, we would have known he was bad news." Jodie sighed, taking a cigarette out of a pack. "He was cheating on her with one of her friends." Jodie offered a cigarette to Kirsty.

"Oh, no thank you, I don't smoke," she replied. "How long was it going on for?"

"Not sure. After Heidi disappeared and when we found out about him I asked him. He said they hadn't been seeing each other long, probably about a month."

"Did you believe him?" Kirsty stopped writing and looked at Jodie.

"I don't know to be honest, I could never be sure."

"Where is he now?" Kirsty asked. "Does he still live around here?" Jodie tipped the ash of her cigarette in the ashtray and blew a puff of smoke away.

"No, but his mother still lives at number 42 a few roads away, Berringer Street."

"Ever talk to her?"

"No, I just cross the street if I see her coming. The police said she had a drug problem at the time, she was into cocaine and she kept some bad company. You know for years I kept on at them saying maybe it was one of them that took her, maybe she knew something about it. They said they questioned her a couple of times though, and she didn't know anything."

Kirsty wrote down what Jodie was saying. She stopped and tapped her pen against her lip thoughtfully. "Was it a woman, DCI McColl who you spoke to?" Kirsty asked.

"What? No, it was a bloke, DCI Harold Spencer, he was leading on the case at the time."

"Oh, really? OK, I'm not sure he's still with the force anymore."

"No, he left a few years back, took early retirement, was moving to the Isle of Wight, I recall. Think he died soon after retirement though, car accident," Jodie said as she finished her cigarette. "Do want a drink or anything?" she asked, getting up and going to the kitchen.

"Oh, just some water please," Kirsty replied.

After a few minutes Jodie came back into the living room and sat down. She had a glass of brandy and brought it to her lips. "What about Joe Allington? Did Heidi ever mention him?" Kirsty asked.

"Who?" Jodi looked puzzled.

"Ken Allington's nephew, he was staying with Ken that summer and mixed with that circle of friends."

Jodi's face showed recognition. "Oh yeah, him. Scrawny kid, looked younger than his age. Ken used to take the piss out of him for it," she mused. "Do you know, I'd forgotten about him. That kid was scared of his own shadow. Last I'd heard was that he moved away to America with his mum." Kirsty listened with interest before pressing on.

"Was his mum Ken's sister?"

Jodie sipped her drink, and shook her head, saying, "Half-sister, I don't think they got on that well."

Kirsty frowned. "Did Heidi ever mention Joe or have much to do with him?"

Jodie thought for a few moments. Smoking a cigarette, she tapped her lips thoughtfully.

"Well, not really, think he just latched onto that group of friends while staying in the area over the holidays. There was one thing though that I could never really understand."

Kirsty stopped writing and looked up with interest. "Really? What's that?"

"DCI Spencer thought it wasn't worth pursuing at

the time, said they had other active lines of enquiry of more interest."

Kirsty listened eagerly. "Go on…" she pressed.

"Well, Ken was in the area that night originally. He was seen, a witness placed his car outside the park but it couldn't be corroborated as another witness placed his car outside his house at exactly the same time; the problem was the witness who had originally said he had seen the car outside the park was 'an unreliable witness'. Apparently he had been drinking whilst on prescription drugs. Then all of a sudden the other witness came forward and made a statement confirming that Ken's car was outside his house all evening and so he couldn't have been at the park. After that the police were no longer interested in Ken."

"What happened with the other alibi?" Kirsty asked. Jody took a puff on her cigarette and blew it away, tapping ash into the ashtray as she did so.

"The police said that Ken was at home at the time his neighbour saw him getting out of his car that night. The car was there for the rest of the evening." Jodie shrugged.

"Which neighbour was it? Do you know the name?" Kirsty asked.

"Police said they couldn't tell me that, said it been

checked and it was true as far as they were concerned. The sighting of the car outside the park was what went on record as the other statement was retracted. They said they couldn't be sure." Kirsty scribbled this information down on her notepad; her mind was racing.

"What was Heidi's boyfriend's name again?" she asked as she wrote.

"Kieran, his mum's name is Sandra Kennedy and she was seeing that bar owner Ken at the time."

Kirsty stopped and looked up, surprised. "Really? I didn't know that."

Jodie continued, "Yeah. Don't talk now as far as I know, it wasn't a nice break-up all accounts."

"How did you find that out? I didn't even know they had been in a relationship at the time."

Jodie laughed and coughed at the same time. Waving her hand with the cigarette, she said, "No, no, no honey, a relationship? Well, I wouldn't go that far." Jodie took a sip of her drink "They were just having a fling, he was selling coke at the time, he was her bit of rough, and Sandra always had an eye for nice things, things that cost money. Sandra would sell coke for Ken in order to get it. Fancy holidays, nice clothes, you name it. The woman was shameless. When Heidi took up with her son Kieran she should have known he would be bad news, but I guess she liked him," Jodie said sadly. "We didn't know anything about them seeing each other until after Heidi had disappeared." Kirsty listened with interest.

"So how did Ken end up in a fling with Sandra? Wasn't she married at the time?"

Jodie shrugged. "Guess so, but her old man was never about, always in and out of prison. Ken took her under his wing, he loved her Kieran like his own son."

Kirsty struggled to get back to the point. *Why is this relevant?* she thought to herself.

Jodie went on, "Ken's half-sister Carly was Joe Allington's mum. Ken always compared Joe to Kieran and played them off against each other. Sandra lived across the street from Ken, that's how they met, then when Joe stayed with Ken that summer he started hanging around with Kieran."

Kirsty thought for a moment. "Could it have been Sandra who gave Ken an alibi?"

Jodie nodded in agreement. "Yeah, I thought the same thing at the time, but Spencer wouldn't say who it was." Kirsty wrote this down. She wondered more about DCI Harold Spencer and what he may have known before he died. She wrote this down, along with 'who was the unreliable witness who retracted their statement from the park?' Seeing Kirsty wondering and reading her mind, Jodie interrupted her thoughts. "That was Frank. Frank Musgrove."

Chapter 8

Kirsty parked the car across the street from Ken's bar a while later. As she got out, Kirsty locked the car, looked both ways and crossed the road. It was earlier than she had planned to meet Matt but she had decided to drive straight there and sound Ken out.

As it was still early the bar was empty, apart from a couple who were sat down the far end on the left side in one of the booths. As Kirsty approached the bar, the girl got up and her friend passed her a jacket. "Laters Ken," the guy called out and they walked to the door and left the bar.

"Yeah, see ya," Ken called back turning around from stacking the glasses away on the shelf. "Oh, hiya skwirt," he greeted Kirsty as she walked up to the bar.

"Hi Ken." Kirsty nodded back.

"What you doing here?"

"Oh, I'm meeting Matthew, has he been in yet?" she asked, knowing it was too early for him to have arrived.

"No, not yet, want a soft drink while you're waiting?"

"Er year, sure, go on then." Kirsty climbed onto one of the bar stools and took her bag off her shoulder.

"What time you expecting him in here?" Ken asked as he poured a drink from one of the hoses and placed it on the bar.

"Oh, anytime now," Kirsty replied vaguely.

"You might pick yourself up a fella while you're waiting," he laughed. Kirsty laughed back good humouredly in agreement.

"Is that how you met Sandra?" she asked.

Ken stopped what he was doing and his face clouded over. Carrying on with what he was doing but without looking up responded, "Now why would you be asking a question like that?" Ken was defensive, an interesting reaction, she thought.

"Well you two were seeing each other, right?"

Ken scoffed dismissively. "Well I'm not sure that

would be how I would describe it, the woman went with anyone," he said arrogantly. "Lucky I even looked at her to be honest, don't know what I was thinking." Ken walked off and began unpacking boxes around the back.

Determined not to be fobbed off, Kirsty pressed on. "You were seeing each other for a few weeks, right?"

Ken came around to the other side of the bar and began collecting ashtrays and emptying them into a larger one. As he neared Kirsty he stood close to her and asked, "Why all the questions?" with a smile but confrontationally.

"I'm just making conversation," she replied innocently. But Ken smelled a rat and the smile disappeared.

"Who have you been talking to?" he asked, beginning to sound aggressive. Realising the game was up Kirsty dropped a bombshell. "What's up, Ken, you got something to hide?"

With that, Ken slammed the ashtrays down on the bar. "You what? You little bitch."

Kirsty suddenly felt very out of her depth and decided to take the bull by the horns; if this was going one way she figured she might as well get some answers.

"You wasn't at home the night Heidi Perthwaite disappeared, were you Ken?"

Ken's eyes widened with anger and he grabbed Kirsty by the arm. "Get out, get out now, you little bitch. You don't know what you're talking about."

"Where is she, Ken? Where is she?" Kirsty's fear was suddenly overtaken by anger. "It was you that murdered Molly, wasn't it? It was you!"

With that, Ken shoved his face into Kirsty's and shouted, "I never touched your sister! Molly was just fine when she left here Christmas Eve!" Spittle spurted from Ken's lips as he shouted in Kirsty's face.

Just then the door swung open, and a voice shouted, "Hey Ken, get off her!" With that, a pair of hands broke them apart. Ken looked up to see Marlon stood there with a couple of his university friends behind him. "Everything OK, darling?" Marlon asked Kirsty. Shaking, she looked up at Marlon, before she could answer, Ken responded.

"Yeah, sure it is Marlon, aren't they, Kirsty? Just a misunderstanding, I was just playing." He smiled cheerily. "Now what can I get you? It's on the house." But Marlon did not break his stare from Kirsty's, suddenly struck by how vulnerable and beautiful she was, as she sat there in stunned silence.

Finding her voice, Kirsty stammered, "Yes, yes I'm fine, everything's fine."

"Can I get you a drink?" Marlon asked.

"Sure, I'll have a bottle of beer," she replied.

Ken was back around the other side of the bar; he opened a bottle of beer and passed it silently across to Marlon, who passed it to Kirsty. She picked up the bottle and started sipping from it. Ken had not argued back about her age; she knew she was onto something but the moment had passed to press on, it would keep. She smiled gratefully at Marlon.

"You're that girl, Molly's sister, aren't you?" he asked, looking at her intently.

"Yes, that's right," she replied. "Ken was just telling me how Molly was fine when she left here on Christmas Eve."

"That's right, she was, I saw her leave," Marlon replied. Kirsty looked at Marlon, her eyes desperate to know more. "Guys, go take a seat in one of the booths, I'll come and join yous in a bit," Marlon said to his friends. Taking a seat on the bar stool next to Kirsty's, he went on. "Molly was fine when she left here, Ken asked her to stay on for a bit later but she wanted to go home, said she was tired or something, I saw her leave."

"Then what? What happened next? Did you see anyone go after her?" Kirsty pressed on.

"No, as we left to go to a house party straight after," Marlon said, thinking back to Ryan chatting to Molly on the way home. He thought about his recent exchange with Ryan. Marlon was unsure of what to say; his voice trailed off. Kirsty looked at Marlon waiting for him to go on. "One of my mate's parents were out Christmas Eve so he had a party."

"Did you see anyone hanging around the bar that night?"

Ken came over then and interrupted. "Here," he said, passing over a couple more beers. "That needs to be your last alcoholic drink or I could lose my licence, young lady."

"Pity that's not all you could lose, isn't it Ken?" Kirsty replied acidly. With that, Ken backed off.

Marlon laughed. "Remind me not to get on the wrong side of you!" he said with a chuckle, shaking his head. "So what's your problem with Ken anyway?" Marlon asked with interest.

Kirsty laughed begrudgingly, then said seriously, "I don't trust him, I never have, and I never will."

He shook his head but held her gaze. "I'm Marlon

by the way."

"Kirsty," she replied and nodded, taking a sip of her drink.

"So how comes you're all alone tonight, Kirsty?" Marlon asked curiously.

"I'm supposed to be meeting my brother Matt, got here early," she said, checking her watch. It was 7.40pm. "He'll be here in twenty minutes or so."

"Well in that case, mind if I have a drink with you and keep you company while you wait?" he grinned.

"Sure, OK," Kirsty replied with a warm smile.

As they chatted for a while, Ken walked over to Lucy, who had just arrived to start her shift. "Mind the bar, will you for a minute?" She nodded, saying nothing. Going to the end of the bar, he pulled his mobile off the lead where it was charging, and texted Ryan. "WHERE ARE YOU MATE? MARLON'S MAKING NEW FRIENDS WAITING FOR YOU." With that he sent another text. "THAT SYMMONDS GIRL IS KEEPING HIM COMPANY."

Ryan was at home in his kitchen when he received the text message. He jumped up with a start in mid conversation with his dad about football. Brian was enjoying a rare catch-up with his son, when Ryan's attention was suddenly distracted. "Dad, I got to go, sorry, something's come up."

"Oh sure son, is everything OK?" Brian asked with concern. "What's the sudden rush?"

Ryan laughed, a dry sarcastic sound. "Oh you know, got to see a man about a dog." With that, Ryan grabbed his jacket and was out of the front door before his dad could ask anything else.

Matt was at home, getting ready to meet Kirsty. Oliver was lying on the sofa watching TV. "Fancy coming for a drink? Said I'd meet Kirsty," Matt asked Oliver.

"Nah, you're alright, can't be bothered," he responded lazily. "Where's Dad?" Oliver asked.

"Oh, gone down the Red Lion. I think there's a match on."

Oliver sat up and stretched. "Oh really? Who's playing?" he asked, his mind already made up that he would go down there.

"Don't know, if you fancy a pint come with me to Ken's bar."

"Nah, you're alright, thanks for the offer though," he responded. "I might go down and catch the match with Dad." Oliver sat up and pulled his socks on.

Matt was sorting his collar out in the mirror on the wall above the fireplace.

"You two seem to be spending a lot of time together lately, how does Dad seem to you, how's he doing?" Matt asked, turning to look at Oliver.

"Yeah, he's OK," Oliver replied, picking up his cigarettes and lighting one. He offered one to Matthew, with his lighter. Matthew took a cigarette, lit it and passed the lighter back. "I'm going to catch up with Dad, going to grab a shower first. You go, I'll catch up with you later."

"Alright, see you later." Matthew picked up his wallet and keys.

As soon as the door shut behind him Oliver called his dad on his mobile. The phone rang a few times, then went onto voicemail. "Dad, it's me. Just to let you know I'm coming down to meet you, be there in an hour." He stubbed out his cigarette, and went up to take a shower.

Ryan walked into Ken's bar and grimaced at the sight that greeted him. Marlon was still sat at the bar beside Kirsty. Just as Ken's text message had sounded; they were too cosy for his liking. Kirsty was laughing at something Marlon was saying, Marlon was sat beside her and was leaning on the back of her chair with one arm. They were deeply engrossed in animated conversation and didn't notice him arriving.

Walking over, Ryan said loudly, "Hey buddy, what's going on? We rolling tonight or what?"

Marlon stopped mid-conversation. "Er, you what? Thought we were staying here for the night. The guys are over there." Marlon nodded to the left end booth where the rest of his friends were.

Ryan stood in between their chairs so Marlon had to move his arm. Turning his back to Kirsty and facing Marlon he replied, "No, no, that was earlier, there's been a change of plan, mate, there's a house party on the campus."

"Oh really?" Marlon sounded surprised.

"Yeah, one of Chloe's friends is having a get-together, thought we should go and see what it's like."

Marlon frowned and laughed at the same time. "Since when did you ever want to show an interest in Chloe's friends?" He laughed and looked at Kirsty.

"It's OK, you go," Kirsty said dismissively. "My brother will be here soon anyway."

"Well I'm a man of my word, so I'll wait with you until he arrives," Marlon said, looking at Ryan, who breathed irritably.

"Fine," he replied. "Ken, get me a beer please."

"Coming right up," Ken replied, looking at Ryan then back at Kirsty and Marlon, then at Ryan warily.

Matt arrived after another ten minutes by which time the trio were talking about game shows. Ryan had pulled up a chair in between them and was dominating the conversation by reminiscing about the eighties. "'Bullseye' seriously though, who thought that shit up?" Ryan laughed.

"Someone with a sense of humour!" Kirsty replied. On her third beer, she was feeling quite tipsy; she took a sip of her drink. "Can you imagine the opposite, if you didn't win? Look at all the shame and embarrassment your friends and family who would feel, lucky for you, you did OK – today!" They laughed together at Kirsty's joke. Ryan made eye contact with Kirsty.

"So erm, what time did your brother say he would be meeting you? It's just we need to be making tracks, Marlon." As Ryan said that, Matt entered the bar and Kirsty turned as she heard the door go.

"Oh look, there he is now! Matt; over here!"

Matt walked over and saw Kirsty waving emphatically. He eyed up the two guys sitting with his younger sister. "Hi Kirsty, who's this?" he asked good naturedly with interest. Recognising Marlon from campus, they nodded at each other.

"Oh, this is Marlon, and this is Ryan. Guys, this is my brother Matt."

"Hey, you go to the university on the Greenwood campus?" Marlon replied, shaking Matt's hand.

"Yeah, thought I recognised you," Matt agreed.

"Hi buddy." Ryan shook Matt's hand. "Come on Marlon, let's go." Ryan got up to leave.

"Well why don't you come with us, to the party on Greenwood?" Marlon asked brightly. "You're bound to know people there."

Hiding his initial reaction, Ryan Cooley replied, "Well, no, actually, you know what Chloe's mates are like, they can be right bitchy."

Not keen on going, Matthew replied, "Yeah, it's cool, don't worry about it. Kirsty we're only staying for a couple of drinks tonight anyway, some other time though."

"Yeah sure, some other time," Kirsty agreed, looking at Marlon.

"Oh, OK," Marlon replied, clearly disappointed. "Can I get your number? I'd like to take you out sometime, if that's OK?"

Kirsty smiled, blushing slightly. "Sure." She felt the brazen confidence of the alcohol, took a pen from her bag and wrote down her number on a cardboard beer coaster. As she passed it to Marlon, he smiled, pleased with himself, "Nice!" and laughed. "So I'll call you…"

After Ryan and Marlon had left the bar, Matthew looked at his little sister. "What?" she asked defensively. "I'll be seventeen in a few weeks' time."

"Yeah and he's like nineteen now," Matt replied. "What do you think Dad's going to say when he finds out?"

But Kirsty shook her head. "Oh lighten up, Matt, I need to have room to breathe, and I like him. He seems nice, so yeah, I'm going to go on a date with him."

At the house party, Ryan was bored. Chloe and her college friends were all out in force, all thick makeup and bomber jackets. They were discussing an eclectic mix of music, politics and the environment. Ryan was almost bored out of his mind. "You see man, I knew we should have brought them with us, these people are so dry," Marlon complained.

Looking at him, Ryan replied, "By 'them', I take it you mean that girl Kirsty?"

Marlon smiled to himself. "Well, yeah." Ryan was irritated but tried to play down his irritation.

"She's not your type. You'll have a much better chance of scoring and getting laid with one of these girls."

"What if I don't want to?" Marlon replied. "I mean it Ryan, I like the girl. I'm going to take her out, on a proper date." Ryan laughed, good humoured, but inside he was seething. If only he had got to the bar sooner.

Chapter 9

Oliver arrived at the Red Lion pub just after 8.30pm. He saw his dad sitting in his usual spot, over on the right-hand side, by the window. "Hey Dad, what's happening?"

Looking up from his newspaper as his son sat down, John took a sip from his pint. "Just catching the game, what you doing here?"

"Fancied a pint. Want another?" John nodded at Oliver who went up to the bar, returning a short while later with two pints.

He sat down and checked nobody was within earshot, before asking in a low voice, "Any more news on the shooting?" covering his mouth with his pint glass as he asked. John grimaced, not removing his eyes from the football match on the large screen.

"No. And I don't want it mentioned in public again," he warned Oliver icily.

Saying nothing, but taking another sip of his pint, Oliver picked up the newspaper his dad had been reading. He picked up his pint and took a gulp of the cool, froth-topped pint. "That's nice!" he said as he took another gulp. Suddenly, something caught his attention and he placed the pint down on the beer coaster on the wooden table. He noticed a small article on the front page with the heading 'Shooter Still Not Found' with a narrative leading to page five in the newspaper. Oliver flicked through to page five and folded over the newspaper as he read. However, when he got to the page where the article should have been there was a corner section missing in the newspaper. John covered his mouth with his pint as he spoke. "It's gone. I removed it before you ask," reading Oliver's mind. Casually, Oliver folded the newspaper back up and went back to his pint. "Where are the others?" John asked, changing the subject.

"Kirsty went out earlier, think she was meeting Matthew over at Ken's bar." John put his pint down and lit up a cigarette.

"Keep an eye on her, I don't want her finding out

anything about match night." Oliver nodded.

"How's work?"

"Yeah, alright, we might be getting a big contract. Speaking of which, isn't it about time you stopped mucking around changing firms all the time?" Oliver grimaced. The idea of having to get up each day to go to the place where he was told what to do and when to do it just wasn't appealing. Oliver had never been great at holding down a job. Then when Molly died he had just gone back to one of his preferred professions, serving up, selling weed. However, even that work had dried up recently as he had been smoking most of the profits. "You need to sort yourself out, son, get a job, find yourself a girl, and settle down," John said to his son affectionately. "You ain't getting any younger."

"Says you," Oliver responded, and laughed. John laughed too. He shook his head, admitting defeat. "So Dad, when you going to get yourself back out there? Mum wouldn't want you to be on your own. You should start seeing someone."

John smiled, but Oliver's gaze had made him feel uncomfortable. Since Lisa had died there had been a few women over the years, but none could hold a torch to his darling wife. John knew that his son had his best interests at heart and shrugged casually. "Yeah, maybe." He stood up and clapped. "Goal!" he shouted at the TV screen, relieved to have a reason to change the subject.

*

"Come on Kirsty, I think I'd better be getting you home." Matt spoke to his sister, noticing the couple of drinks she had consumed since his arrival had gone to her head.

"What? No way," she argued. Then she giggled. "You're such a spoil sport, I'm just getting started. Besides, this is fun."

Matt was worried about what his father would say if he saw the state his sister was getting into, and even more so, that he would get the blame. "Kirsty, come on, let's get you home. You can pick the car up tomorrow. I'm not having you driving."

Kirsty laughed. "Next you'll be telling me you're calling the cops on me for underage drinking! Hahahahaha!"

Matt laughed reluctantly. "Don't tempt me! Well come on, at least have a soft drink?"

"Go on then, I'll have a Coca-Cola."

"Ken, can I get two Cokes when you're ready?"

Ken looked over and nodded, his eyes on Kirsty for longer than necessary. Matt had noticed the atmosphere between Ken and Kirsty. "Has something happened between you two?" he asked. However, Kirsty didn't answer. Matt watched his sister as she was staring coldly at Ken, in response. Ken looked uncomfortable as he was packing bags of crisps into boxes. "Kirsty, what's going on?" he asked again.

Finally after a few seconds she responded with a firm, "Nothing."

Deciding to park the subject for now, Kirsty decided in her drunken haze that she wanted to enjoy her brother's company. She was certain that Ken was hiding something and was not going to let it go that easily. However, for now, she changed the subject. "Where's Dad and Oliver tonight?"

"They're at the Red Lion catching the match. Are you OK? I'm worried about you."

She stumbled off the stool, "I'm fine, just going to the little girl's room. Watch my bag for me."

"Sure," Matt said, watching her go. She walked off towards the ladies', which were around the right side of the bar. Ken came over to Matt after she had walked off. She was learning fast not to show her emotions in front of her dad and her brothers. Since their mum had died they had all become overprotective, but since Molly things had only got worse and she was beginning to feel a bit suffocated.

Putting the two Cokes on the bar, Ken said to Matt, "Son, I don't think your dad would be too happy about the state of your sister tonight, might want to think about getting her off home."

Matt looked up and nodded in agreement. "Yeah, sure Ken. Hey, is everything alright? I mean has something happened between you two? Things seem a bit hostile."

Ken cleared away their empty glasses. "Yeah everything's fine, she's just had a bit too much to drink, take her home."

Kirsty came out of the cubicle and went over to wash her hands. She washed her hands and stared at her reflection in the mirror above the sink. Her mascara had smudged under her blue eyes, so she splashed some water on her face and took a paper towel from the dispenser and wiped over her face. Suddenly realising how much she had had to drink she was beginning to feel nauseous. She splashed more water over her face and took another hand towel. As she wiped her face with the paper towel she heard laughter as two girls entered the ladies' behind her. She turned around and there were two teenage girls coming in. One went into a cubicle and the other went over to the mirror and started applying lipstick. They continued their chatter as Kirsty went to leave. "Hey, you're Molly's sister aren't you?" The girl had turned away from the mirror and was looking at her.

"Yes, I am, why?"

The girl looked awkward as she said, "I'm so sorry to hear what happened."

Kirsty had a lump in her throat. "Thanks. See you around." Kirsty left the toilets and walked back over to her brother. "I don't feel so good, let's go home."

Matt picked up her satchel and passed Kirsty her jacket. "Sure." They put on their jackets and walked over to the door. As they were leaving the girls came out of the toilets. One of them stopped as she saw them leaving, but then continued after her friend who walked back over to one of the booths to join their friends.

Walking up the road Kirsty said, "Did you know that Ken was in a relationship with the mother of the boyfriend of that girl Heidi who disappeared all these years ago?"

Walking side by side, Matt looked up at her and nodded. "Er, yeah, I think so."

Kirsty was surprised. "Oh, how did you know that?"

Puzzled, Matt shook his head. "Er, I don't know, think maybe Oliver mentioned it, he was working at Ken's bar around that time and he knew about it."

Kirsty was stunned into silence. If anyone had more information on Ken's movements around that time it would be Oliver. If Oliver was working at the bar when Heidi disappeared, maybe he had seen something but didn't realise the significance of it. Kirsty was suddenly desperate to see Oliver. "Hey, shall we go to the Red Lion and catch up with Dad and Oliver?"

Matt laughed. "Uh-uh, no way, there's only one place I'm taking you to, and that's home."

Chapter 10

It was just after 9.30am on Sunday morning when the doorbell went. John, who had been sitting in the armchair reading through the morning's papers, got up and picked up his coffee. It was unusual to receive visitors so early on a Sunday morning. Curiously sipping at his drink, he walked out of the lounge and over to the front door. As he pulled the door towards him, he found a fairly striking-looking middle-aged woman standing on the doorstep; she was wearing a black trouser suit and had short cropped brown hair with blue eyes. Beside her was a younger-looking male companion, John recognised them both from the funeral. "Yes, can I help you?" he enquired. Flashing her police badge, DCI McColl introduced herself and Sergeant Bates. Feeling his blood run cold, John stepped aside and let the officers through. "Er, straight ahead, first on the right." John directed them to the living room, walking in behind them; he folded the papers up and sat down in the armchair, and the officers sat down on the sofa, and made themselves comfortable. Sally McColl took in her surroundings; the living room was tidy, everything was in its place, from the DVDs on their rack, to the way John had folded the papers and put them to one side. There were several pictures on the walls and opposite where they were sitting was a large fireplace, over which hung a mirror which reflected the light from the window to the right, and gave the room an open airy feel.

"Can I get you a tea or coffee?" John asked them both.

McColl shook her head. "No, I'm fine thanks." Bates also shook his head in response.

"Thank you for seeing us, we just wanted to update you with the progress of our investigation," McColl said. John felt himself relax a little, if this was about Molly's murder they mustn't be here about the shootings, he thought to himself. McColl went on, "So I had a visit from your other daughter, Kirsty isn't it?"

"Yes," John responded, surprised.

"You didn't know she had come down to the station?" McColl observed his reaction.

John shook his head, admitting this was new information he wasn't aware of. McColl stopped herself from showing her amusement.

"Yes, she wanted to ask about the disappearance of a young girl who went missing a few years back, Heidi Perthwaite. Your daughter believes this could be linked to what happened to Molly."

"Oh, I see," John replied, putting his cup down and scratching his chin thoughtfully. "Could she be right?"

McColl shifted in her seat. "I'm unable to comment at this stage, but I do have some questions for you." Bates silently observed McColl, and her body language. Usually McColl was unfazeable; however, he noticed McColl appeared a little uncomfortable in this situation. Gaining some composure, McColl went on. "Mr Symmonds…"

"Er, call me John," he replied, picking his coffee back up and sipping it.

"John, how well do you know Ken Allington?"

John immediately felt his back go up. Was Ken linked to this? "Well, my wife knew Ken quite well, they grew up together in Edenbridge, she passed away some years ago. Then my older son Oliver did some shifts at his bar when he was at college, as did Molly…" John's voice trailed off.

"John, I understand this may be difficult for you, but I do need to ask these questions, we could go down the station if you'd prefer."

John choked back tears but joked, "Am I under arrest?" He brushed the tears away with the back of his hand. McColl felt a surge of sympathy for the broken man in front of her. He was probably a very good-looking man in his younger days, still was in fact, but he had been living in the shadows of grief for many years, and they had clearly taken their toll on him.

McColl gave John a couple of minutes to contain himself. She looked around the living room and looked at the photos that decorated the walls. There were photos of them as a family, when the children were young, John's wife Lisa was sitting by a poolside with John in one of them, and the kids were in the water splashing as the photo had been taken; it was a moment in time that held such joy, and McColl felt a lump rise in her throat. She looked at the other pictures, one in particular stood out; it was of two teenage girls of similar age, both with brown hair, one with straight hair, the other curly. Molly and Kirsty, she correctly guessed to herself.

"That was Molly's 18th birthday party, taken shortly before what had happened," John said, noticing McColl staring at the photograph. "They were so close when they were younger, argued and bickered as they got older though, as siblings do. They had different interests as they grew up so I don't have many photos of them together from when they got older, so that's a rare one, and the last photo of them taken together." John fought back tears and looked away.

"How were you when Molly started working at Ken's bar?" McColl asked. John's face turned to steel; there was a moment's silence before he answered.

"I knew it was a bad idea. I should have put my foot down."

"Why didn't you?" Bates chipped in. They both looked up at Bates, and McColl glared at him. Bates, realising he had been a bit abrupt, tried to backtrack. "What I meant was, why did you allow her to work there? You must have trusted the guy – Ken?"

John just looked at Bates and shrugged. "I had no reason not to." John went on, "My wife Lisa, she knew Ken for years, they knocked about together when they grew up, you see. Ken's uncle had some farmland in

Edenbridge, they spent summers knocking about there with friends. They both grew up in Kent, there's not much there, Lisa's parents moved to London and Lisa transferred to my secondary school, that's how we met. Ken moved into the area a year or so after, bought his bar and the rest is history."

"Does Ken's family still live in Edenbridge?" McColl asked.

"No, I think they passed away a few years ago and the land was sold. That's how Ken had money to buy the bar."

"Did Matthew ever work for Ken?"

"No, he works part time in the local garage – Essex Pride Autos. Started there just before my mother-in-law Elaine passed away, she knew the guy who owned it and put a word in for him. Got Matt some Saturdays there, just basic stuff, helping out with MOTs. He's at uni at the moment so still does shifts there around his studies."

McColl noted this down. "What about Oliver? Does he still do shifts at Ken's bar?"

John shook his head. "No, Ken sacked Oliver because he was too unreliable."

"When did that happen?" McColl asked with interest.

"Around seven years ago, that'd be around 1990."

McColl stopped writing and looked up. *That would have been around the time of Heidi's disappearance*, she thought. "Is Oliver around now?" McColl asked.

"Erm, I think he's still asleep, want me to wake him?" John asked.

"Yes please, I'd just like to ask him a few questions, it shouldn't take too long." Bates looked at McColl curiously, wondering where all this was heading.

John got up, walked out of the room, and up the stairs. He knocked on his son's bedroom door and opened it. Matt was still asleep in his bed over by the window. However, Oliver's bed looked like it had not been slept in. Heading back downstairs, John went back into the living room. "I'm sorry but he's not here, looks like Oliver didn't come home last night."

*

An hour later, Kirsty woke up and went downstairs. She went into the kitchen to make herself a coffee; her head was heavy and her eyes felt dry. She splashed some cold water onto her face and was wiping her face on a towel from the radiator when Matt joined her. "How's the head this morning?" he asked, grinning.

"It's fine thanks, where's Oliver?"

"I don't know, think he hooked up with Karen last night, they were texting each other." Kirsty was surprised, they had broken up ages ago and she wasn't aware they were even back on speaking terms.

Just then, her mobile bleeped. Kirsty went and sat on a stool at the breakfast bar, and detached her mobile from where it was charging. She smiled as she read the message, it was from Marlon. "HI GORGEOUS, FANCY A COFFEE LATER AT DORIS CAFE?"

Kirsty typed back, "SURE, LET ME KNOW WHAT TIME X." She waited a few seconds before the response came.

"BE THERE AROUND 1PM X"

Kirsty texted back a response then went back to her coffee. Marlon smiled as he put his phone in his pocket. Frank looked at his nephew. "Oh, I know that look, so who is she?" He smiled.

"She is none of your business," he laughed in response. "I'll tell you once we've been out a few times."

Chapter 11

Karen lay on her side, staring at the wall. She felt Oliver stirring beside her and quickly closed her eyes to hide her discomfort. Oliver, oblivious to Karen's reaction, slid one arm around her naked waist, under the duvet. He pulled her towards him and began nuzzling her neck.

What was she thinking texting him last night? Karen berated herself. Splitting up with Oliver had been a long time coming, then when Molly was murdered Karen had put it off, though deep down she knew their relationship had been over for a long time. It had never seemed like the right time to cut loose and end it with Oliver. After she found out about Molly, Karen admitted to herself the irritation of having to stay in the relationship had got to her and she had used the fact that Oliver had turned to drink to her advantage. *So now what?* she thought to herself.

"Morning babe," Oliver said as he kissed her neck. "You awake?"

Karen pretended to remain sleeping. Oliver sat up and walk over to the bathroom. As soon as the door had closed, Karen threw the duvet over her head. *What have I done now?* she thought to herself. Taking a deep breath, quickly Karen jumped out of bed and threw on her dressing gown. Oliver came out of the bathroom; he grinned as he saw her up out of bed.

"Oh, so you are awake!" He pulled Karen into his arms and kissed her passionately.

Pulling away, Karen said, "Look, last night was great – amazing in fact – but…"

"But what?" Oliver looked at her.

Unable to hide how she felt, Karen responded, "Look, I'm sorry. I just think this was a bad idea." Hurt beyond belief, Oliver frowned.

"What? I mean, why? I thought we were going to give things another shot?"

Karen went over to check her phone. "Look, I

need to get going; can we talk about this later?" she asked, desperate to get herself out of the situation. Walking over to the bathroom, she looked back, with a pang of conscience and said, "Look, I'll call you later yeah? I need to shower. You can see yourself out, right?"

Dazed, Oliver nodded. "Yeah, sure," he said to the bathroom door as it closed. Oliver stared at the door, and fought back tears. Slowly, he gathered his things and got dressed. Karen took a longer shower than usual, hoping that by the time she came out, Oliver would have taken the hint and be gone. She had hoped right.

*

Matthew was heading out the door to meet up with some friends. As he picked up his jacket and opened the front door, Oliver came in. "Oh, hi," Matt said as they bumped into each other in the doorway. Oliver grunted in response and disappeared up the stairs. *What's wrong with him?* Matthew looked at Kirsty as he wondered, leaving the house. Kirsty shrugged back and turned to stare after her older brother as he disappeared up the staircase.

Oliver went into his and Matthew's bedroom and closed the door behind him. He threw himself down on his bed by the wall over by the window. As he lay there, facing the wall, there was a gentle knocking on the bedroom door. At first he didn't answer it and just hoped his sister would go away. Kirsty waited and then tried again, knocking on the door gently, half expecting to get her head bitten off. Reluctantly, Oliver sighed. "Come in," he called over his shoulder, continuing to face the wall.

Kirsty opened the door slowly, and put her head around the gap. "Hey, you OK?" she asked.

"I'm fine," he replied. Turning around, he sat back up. "What's up?" he asked. Kirsty came in and sat on the edge of her brother's bed.

"We had some visitors earlier, thought you might want to know. They came around before you arrived home." Approaching the subject delicately, she waited for curiosity to get the better of Oliver.

"Oh really?" he replied, barely hiding his boredom.

"Yes, it was the police," Kirsty said, knowing it would get Oliver's attention. Oliver sat up straighter, his mind immediately going to the shootings.

"Oh really? What did they want?" he asked, trying to calm his nerves and racing heart. His mind was also racing, and he was beginning to wonder where his dad was.

"Yeah, they wanted to ask you about when you used to work at Ken's bar."

Oliver was surprised to hear this. *What is this about?* he wondered to himself.

"Why did you stop working there again?"

Oliver was temporarily distracted and didn't understand the question for a few seconds. "Huh? Oh, Ken sacked me," he replied, gathering some composure before continuing. "I was late a few times, so he got rid of me, told me I wasn't needed anymore. I wouldn't mind but that was one of the few times I was actually on time that day!" Oliver laughed at the memory.

Kirsty wondered what the real reason was for her brother being sacked that day, but kept her own counsel. She could recall her brother had always been a bad time keeper, it was in his nature. Something told Kirsty there was another reason Ken had let Oliver go that day. As she pondered on this, Oliver's slumped shoulders dragged her attention away from her thoughts. "What's up? I can tell something's wrong," she asked. "Where were you last night? Matt said you might have stayed at Karen's, you guys back on?"

Oliver's face turned to stone as he clenched his fists. "I'd rather not discuss it if it's all the same to you, sis. So, what did the police say?" he asked, changing the subject back again.

Kirsty felt her brother's disappointment but knew it was pointless pursuing the discussion if Oliver didn't want to talk about it; she knew it meant that Karen had called it a day again. In a way, she could see why things were unlikely to ever work out between them, but feeling a natural allegiance to her brother she still felt angry. Karen was an ambitious, beautiful girl who had always gone for what she wanted in life. Oliver procrastinated, and had always been a bit too laid back for Karen, who was not the type of girl to be tied down young. Maybe one day they would find their way back to each other when Oliver had grown up a bit and Karen was ready to settle down. Suddenly remembering she was going to meet Marlon for coffee, she slowly stood up again. "I'm going out in a bit so I'll catch you later, will you be OK?" Kirsty asked her brother.

"Yeah, I'll be fine, just need to get some sleep, didn't get much last night." He forced a chuckle.

"I'll see you later then."

*

Marlon checked his phone again as he sat at a table by the window of Doreen's café. He nervously looked out the window up the street; it was pouring down outside, and he was starting to doubt that Kirsty would show up. "Hey Marlon," Doreen said as she came over and wiped down the table. The usual stream of Sunday lunchtime people, drinking their tea and eating a mix of fry-ups, and bacon or sausage sandwiches. The smell was making Marlon hungry, but he wanted to wait until Kirsty arrived before ordering food. "I'm good thanks, I will order, just waiting for someone to arrive first."

Doreen smiled a knowing smile. "No problem, just give me a shout whenever you're ready."

As Doreen walked away, Kirsty came into the café; she pulled her hood back as she came over. "Hey, you alright?"

Marlon smiled. Kirsty was wearing a red hooded coat, jeans and jumper. It was raining outside, so she draped her wet coat on the back of the chair and sat down opposite Marlon. "I'm great now you're here, was getting a bit worried you were going to stand me up," he laughed honestly. Kirsty felt a pang of sympathy for the young man sat at the table in front of her.

"Well I said I'd meet you, so here I am," she smiled. Marlon grinned back.

"So what are you having? My treat," Marlon asked, checking out the breakfast and lunch menu.

"Oh I'll just have a coffee thanks," she replied. Marlon looked disappointed.

"Oh, go on, eat something, I'm starving and I hate eating alone. Besides, you were late so you've got some making up to do."

Kirsty laughed good-naturedly. "Oh go on then, I'll have a bacon sandwich," she chuckled.

"Doreen, we're ready for two fry-ups when you're ready."

"Marlon!" Kirsty laughed in mock horror. "Just a bacon sandwich for me please!" she called over her shoulder, but kept her eyes on Marlon.

"And two coffees!" he called after. Then mouthed, 'Coffee OK?' Kirsty nodded and laughed. Marlon beamed back at her. "So, how's things, what you been up to?" he asked.

"Oh, this and that," Kirsty replied, suddenly remembering her birthday which was coming up in the following couple of weeks. "Well, my brother's been on at me to arrange a party. I'll be seventeen the week after next – fourteenth of May."

"Oh really?" Marlon asked with interest. "But

you're not keen?" he observed. She shook her head.

"Not really in the right frame of mind for a party," she said. "What did you do for your seventeenth?" Kirsty asked, deflecting the question.

"Oh, that was ages ago," he laughed.

"How old are you?" she asked.

Marlon blushed. "I'm nineteen," he said, feeling awkward about the age gap between them.

"Oh you're not that much older than me, I started college back in September, I'm not still at school." Hoping it would make Marlon feel at ease, she pushed on. "So how about you?"

Marlon looked at Kirsty and tilted his head to one side. "Do you mean my seventeenth or college?" He laughed.

"Both." She grinned.

"Well for my seventeenth I think I just went for a few beers with my mate Ryan and some of our friends. As for college, I did a year of AS Levels and took the fast track to university."

They leaned back as Doreen brought the coffees over and set the tray down on the table. She removed the cups and took the silver jug and sugar pot of the tray.

"Yeah, I wanted to get it over with so I could get my life started, figured it was the quickest way." He added the milk and two sugars to his coffee and stirred it. Sipping at it, he looked up.

Kirsty smiled at him. "Wow. That's impressive," she admitted, waiting for him to continue.

He blushed again and shrugged. "In my spare time I hang out with friends and work in my uncle's shop to have a bit of my own money."

Kirsty picked up the milk jug and added some to her coffee, stirring whilst listening intently. Marlon was easy to embarrass, he had a childish vulnerability to him which she found drew her to him. It made her want to protect him. "Where's your uncle's shop? What to do you do there?" she asked curiously.

"Oh, it's called Frank's Hardware store, DIY type of stuff, I help out with stock taking, serving customers, taking bulk orders for businesses, that type of stuff. It's OK, I get to hang out with my Uncle Frank, he's a lot older than me, but he's cool. The store's up on the high street." Kirsty nodded. "Look, I heard about what happened to your sister, I was really sorry to hear about it…"

Kirsty's smile faded and his voice trailed off. Kirsty looked down into her coffee, not really seeing it. Regretting his change in subject and cursing himself silently, Marlon stayed quiet. After a brief pause, he poured some more milk into his coffee and added another sugar. "Have there been any leads? Do the police have any idea who's responsible?" Kirsty remained silent and shook her head. Unable to think of what to say, Marlon sipped his coffee and looked out of the window.

"I can see why you thought I wouldn't show." Kirsty said gently, looking out at the rain.

"It there's anything I can do, anything you need, just say," Marlon said in response. Kirsty smiled her thanks. They ate their food when it arrived but the conversation wasn't the same. Marlon was kicking himself for being so insensitive. When it came to time to leave, Kirsty thanked Marlon and crossed the street, getting into her car afterwards. She got her Motorola mobile out of her coat pocket, before driving off, she sent Marlon a text. 'This afternoon was nice, let's meet up again soon x.'

Chapter 12

It was a Monday afternoon in May and DCI McColl was eating a sandwich for lunch at her desk when Bates dropped a file on her desk. "The file on Heidi Perthwaite you asked for," he said.

"Oh, cheers," McColl replied, finishing her sandwich. She picked up her apple and started crunching into it. When she was done, she threw the core into the bin and picked up the file slid it closer to her. Turning the pages on the dusty file, she looked at the photo of the missing girl, which was attached by an old paperclip. Heidi was a pretty girl, her blue eyes danced with happiness as though being told a private joke at the time the photograph was being taken.

McColl turned the pages and read the notes from

the original interview with Ken Allington; he had been at home the night the girl had disappeared, and his car had been parked outside his house all evening. McColl flicked the pages to the notes taken from Frank Musgrove's interview. Frank had originally stated he had seen Ken's car parked outside the park that evening, only later Frank had changed his story to say he had been mistaken. McColl frowned thoughtfully. *Why was this not probed further at the time?* she wondered. Folding the file closed, McColl stood up and grabbed her jacket, pulling one arm in and reaching for the other. She picked up her car keys. "Bates, come on, we need to pay a little visit to Mr Frank Musgrove."

*

Marlon was working out the back doing a stock take at Frank's hardware store. He was standing up the ladder and reading out serial numbers to Frank who was standing at the bottom, completing order forms.

"We need to order more XVY20 Masking Tape, we're always selling out of that stuff."

"OK, thanks, Marlon, I'll put double on the order form to what we usually have, I'm sure it'll come in handy at Christmas time!" Frank laughed, shaking his head as he was writing. "So, you're off out after work tonight?" Frank observed the fresh shaven look and aftershave. "This with your mystery girl?" Marlon chuckled.

"It's no big mystery, I just want to see how it goes first."

Frank raised his eyebrows and looked up at his nephew. "So where you taking her then?"

"We're only going out for something to eat, to the precinct. She's at college today, so I'm meeting her there when she finishes her last class."

"How comes you're being so secretive about it? Must like her a lot?" Frank observed.

Marlon blushed and continued to the next set of half empty boxes. "Yeah, I think she's pretty special," he admitted. The door chimed as someone entered the shop, bringing the conversation to a close. Frank put his pen behind his ear and walked out to the front of the shop.

"Can I help you?" Frank asked, coming around to the till at the counter.

Flashing her badge, DCI Sally McColl introduced herself and Bates. "Mind if we could discuss something with you, Mr Musgrove? It shouldn't take too long."

Frank looked puzzled. "Yeah, sure," he replied, his curiosity written across his face. Bates nodded at Frank.

"Is there somewhere we could talk, away from the shop floor?" he asked.

Marlon joined them and came around by the till, listening to the conversation. "I'll cover the shop if you want to go around the back, Uncle Frank."

"Thanks Marlon, sure, come around this way." Frank led the police officers around the back of the shop to a small room. There was a sink in the corner to the right, and in the corner to the left was an old table, with two hard chairs beside it. Frank sat down on one, DCI McColl took the other. Bates closed the door and stood by the wall, getting his note pad out.

"So," Frank said. "What's this about?" he asked. McColl also got her notepad out and pulled her chair closer to the table before beginning with her questions. She wasn't sure whether this would get them any closer to the truth but there were some things which just didn't add up, and the young girl's recent visit to the station had only prompted her thoughts and previous reservations about the case of Heidi Perthwaite. Most surprising of all was the apparent lack of interest in Frank's original statement being retracted and then changed. McColl couldn't get the nagging feeling out of her mind why this was not explored in more depth at the time of the original investigation.

"So Frank, I wanted to discuss a day with you, which was some time ago now. Almost seven years ago; July 28th 1990, do you recall your movements that day?"

Frank appeared to think for a moment then realisation dawned on him as to why the police were here and what this was all about. "Heidi Perthwaite," Frank said. "So that's why you're here."

"Could you just answer the question please, Frank? Where were you that day?" McColl pushed on. "Could you take us through your day that day please?"

Frank coughed and put his clasped hands on the table. "Sure, well I told that other guy everything at the time," Frank said, shrugging. "Spencer something I think his name was."

"DCI Harold Spencer is no longer with the force so I'm just checking a few facts on some old leads. That's alright with you, isn't it Frank?" McColl asked, smiling, but it did not quite reach her eyes. "So, where were you that day?"

"Do you want me to go through the whole day?"

Frank asked.

"Oh, everything you can remember, Frank, no matter how trivial it may seem we want to know everything." Bates looked at Frank and waited for his response. Frank looked up at Bates, then back at DCI McColl.

"There were a few things you weren't sure about at the time, just wondered if time has helped you have some clarity," McColl said suggestively.

Frank paused. He looked at his hands on the table, thinking back. "Well, in the morning I got up, it was a Sunday so the shop wasn't open. I had been having some problems with the cash register that day so I came down to the shop to take it apart and fixed it. The repair work on it didn't take me that long, but once I got here I ended up staying a couple of hours because I had some things I needed to catch up on, just paperwork and stuff. After I was done here, I went to Doreen's café, had something to eat and drove home afterwards. I got home, had a lie down for an hour or so, watched some TV then my wife did us a Sunday roast later that day. After that we watched a film, it was a country and western with John Wayne, 'The Quiet Man'."

McColl and Bates were writing all this down as

Frank continued.

"I was on some medication at the time because my back had been playing up so I had to go to the pharmacy to pick up my prescription. I decided to walk there, the GP had recommended I kept active to try and help with the pain and to stop my back from seizing up. It was really playing me up that day. So after I'd been to the pharmacy, I crossed over the road and went in the Red Lion for a couple of whiskeys after I'd picked up my prescription. On the way home I cut through the side street by the park, that's when I thought I saw Ken's car as I came past the gate. Turned out I must have been mistaken because Ken's car had been outside his house all evening."

DCI McColl stopped writing and looked up. "Wait, could you backtrack please, Frank?" Frank stopped talking and looked surprised. "In your original statement you said you saw Ken's car and it was empty, what time would this have been around?"

"I guess I saw that car around 7 – 7.30pm, I'd popped into the Red Lion pub for a pint on the way back, I told this all to DCI Spencer, he checked and people saw me there."

"What happened to make you change your statement?" McColl watched Frank carefully.

"Nothing, I just went to the police and said I'd remembered the car was blue."

McColl thought for a moment. Ken's car at the time was a silver Cortina, maybe Frank could have been mistaken in the sunlight, it could have looked blue, it was a summertime evening and this could have been a reason for the uncertainty around the colour of the car which was parked outside the park that evening. But something about this just did not feel right and it seemed like there was something they were missing, so she tried a different approach.

"So Frank, do you make a habit of misleading the police and changing statements?" McColl watched Frank's reaction again carefully. Bates was fascinated, his boss was not usually so provoking.

"Look, I told you all I know, and anyway, I wouldn't have even changed my statement had of that Harold not talked me into it!"

McColl gasped with shock. "What do you mean by that, Frank?" McColl asked on red alert.

"He came to see me a week or so after I gave my statement."

McColl could not believe what she was hearing. She pulled a brown file out of her bag and checked the file for a record of a follow-up conversation, but could find nothing. "When was this, Frank? There's no record in here of this," McColl asked as she flicked through the papers in the file.

"It was the Saturday after the girl went missing. He came up behind me as I was closing the shutters, said he wanted to check a couple of things in my statement, asked if it was OK. I said sure, I'm not exactly going to say no to a detective! We got in my van, he got in the passenger seat and said there was a hold-up with the investigation and there was a chance they could find the girl alive if they could get rid of the red herrings in the case. He kept asking if I was sure of the make of the car and if I was sure I got the colour right. I said, it looked silver but I guess it could have been blue. Spencer said I wasn't to worry and just to pop into the station and update my statement, said it wasn't a big deal and these things happen all the time." McColl and Bates were shocked. "I was on medication at the time and had been drinking, it was an easy mistake to make, and that's what he said."

McColl was incredulous, but composing herself, she closed her notebook and put the file away. "Thank you, Frank, you've been really helpful."

"I hope I'm not in any trouble now, do you think I might have been right in my original statement?"

Frank's face showed his shock and guilt as he began to realise the potential consequences of changing his earlier statement.

"Don't worry, Frank." McColl replied. "We'll get to the truth," she said, looking at Bates as she pulled the strap of her bag onto her shoulder. "Thank you for your time."

*

DCI McColl and Bates left Frank's hardware shop and walked in silence to Bates' car. Bates climbed in the driving seat, and McColl joined him on the passenger side. They sat there and stared out of the window, both lost in their own thoughts. After a couple of minutes, Bates said, "Wow, I didn't see that one coming, boss," McColl said nothing, lost in her own thoughts. "I don't get it though, why did DCI Spencer get Frank to change his statement? It doesn't make sense," he exclaimed, interrupting her thoughts. "Did he have something to hide?"

McColl turned and looked at him. "Makes you wonder, doesn't it?"

Bates shook his head incredulously. They sat there digesting the new possibilities opening up in the investigation. After a few minutes McColl said, "What do you reckon the chances are of it all being linked?"

Bates turned and looked at her; confused, he answered, "All of what?"

"Well, the murder of Molly Symmonds, Heidi's disappearance and the shootings on Rosendale Avenue."

Scratching his chin, Bates shook his head again. "But I thought they found out the shootings were drugs related and it had been handed across to the Narcotics Team?"

"It has," McColl agreed. "But it doesn't change the fact that this could all still be connected. Over the past fifteen years these are the only serious crimes in this area and they are all pretty grim, with questionable motives." Bates put some chewing gum in his mouth and offered one to McColl; she shook her head, declining, and pondering the possibilities as Bates chomped away on his chewing gum.

"What about Harold's car crash? Do you suppose it might not have been an accident, could it have been deliberate?"

McColl mulled the situation over. "Don't know," she said, "could all be unrelated. The accident could have just been a coincidence, but let's not rule anything out at this stage." Bates nodded in agreement, pleased the DI had taken his idea seriously.

"Oh, and Bates?"

"Yes boss?"

"Let's just keep this to ourselves for now, whilst we do a bit of digging."

Bates smiled in agreement, and put the key in the ignition. Driving away they fell back into silence, wondering what these new developments might mean and the potential direction the case was about to take.

Chapter 13

Kirsty was in the living room, lying down on the sofa watching a soap opera on TV. It was early on a Monday evening at the beginning of May 1997 and John was just arriving home from work. Hanging his jacket up, hearing the television on he put his head around the living room door to see who was in.

"You alright love?" John asked, putting his bag down.

"Oh hi Dad, you alright? There's some food in the kitchen for you, made some pasta earlier for us all, there's some vegetables in there to go with it."

Going out to the kitchen John replied, "Thanks love." Dishing himself up some food, John put the kettle on and sat down at the breakfast bar. Kirsty came out to the kitchen and joined him. "Where is everyone?" he asked.

Reaching for two cups from the cupboard, Kirsty replied, "Matt's out, not sure where, he went out after he'd eaten. Oliver's upstairs in his room, want a cuppa?"

"Cheers love, I'll have a tea." Kirsty made them both a drink and pulled one of the tall stools up and sat down at the breakfast bar beside her father. "So, you had any more thoughts about your birthday?" John asked in between mouthfuls of pasta.

"Oh no, not really, can't be bothered to be honest Dad."

John looked at his daughter sadly. "Kirsty, you'll be seventeen, we've got to do something. Oliver said you didn't want a party but maybe it might be nice to have something to look forward to?"

"Oh, I don't know, Dad," Kirsty replied without enthusiasm.

"Well how about we just go for drinks?" John asked.

"Please don't say Ken's bar," she replied, looking at her dad, frowning.

"No? OK, well how about the Red Lion?"

Kirsty sighed. Relenting, she replied, "OK, well, maybe. But it's a bit short notice, doubt many people will come."

"We'll be there, me and your brothers. Come on, what do you say?" John persisted, chomping on his pasta and sipping his tea.

"OK, well can we do it on Friday rather than Saturday? I'd rather be indoors watching TV on Saturday night."

"Sure, I'll let your brothers know and we'll sort something out. Invite some of your friends."

*

It was Wednesday morning when DCI McColl and DI Bates went to see Sandra Kennedy. As the car turned right into Berringer Street they looked at the row of detached houses, counting down the numbers. Number 42 was on the right-hand side. They parked on the right-hand side of the road and noticed the high hedge which was between the pavement and the front garden of the house. DCI McColl looked across the street at the house further up on the left. "That must be Ken Allington's house," Bates said, reading her thoughts. "Will we be popping in for a brew there after?" Bates quipped happily.

McColl stared at the house in consternation. "Not today but maybe another day, when he's home," McColl replied, observing the absence of Ken's car and the front drive being empty. They got out of the car, and Bates locked it with the key as McColl went first and opened the front gate to the garden. The entrance to the house was extraordinary, in the fact that it was on the same street as many other detached houses, but this one, with its high hedge, which arched over the entrance to the front gate, created a guarded, grand entrance. The gate opened onto a pathway which to the left had an immaculate green lawn. There was a flower bed to the right of the path which was well kept and fragrant. The house had a fresh white-painted exterior, and there were clean, pretty net curtains hanging in the windows. DCI McColl and DI Bates made their way slowly up the pathway to the house, taking in their surroundings. There was a heavy brass lion head knocker, hanging on the red front door. It made a loud *rat-a-tat* as McColl knocked on the door. They looked at each other fleetingly with an anxious, apprehensive look, not knowing what would result from this visit.

After a couple of minutes, they heard the sound of light footsteps, making their way to the front door across tiled flooring. As the door opened, a slim, attractive, blonde, middle-aged woman in her late forties greeted them. She was wearing a pink cardigan, and blue denim jeans. The woman scraped her hair behind one ear as she opened the door. A small spaniel appeared beside her and Sandra patted his head. Her smile widened as Sandra Kennedy looked at DI Bates.

Flashing her badge, McColl introduced herself. Bates also flashed his badge. The smile disappeared as quickly as it had arrived. "Can we come in for a quick chat please, Mrs Kennedy?" McColl asked, smiling politely and hiding her amusement at the reaction of their badges.

"What's this about? Have you got a warrant?" the woman replied.

McColl's clipped response was cutting. "No, did we need one? It is Mrs Kennedy, isn't it?"

Nodding, Sandra Kennedy stepped aside to allow them into the house. Waving a hand at the living room door she said, "Please, through here." They entered the living room, with its luxurious soft furnishings, taking a seat on one of two three-seater sofas which sat opposite each other. Between them there was a black marble table which held some magazines in a neat pile, an ashtray and a packet of cigarettes with a lighter placed on the top. Sandra took a seat on the sofa on the opposite side of the table. Taking a cigarette out of the pack, she lit one up and offered them to the inspectors. They both declined.

"So Sandra, thanks for agreeing to speak with us," McColl began.

"Not like I had much choice it would seem." Sandra smiled icily at the police officers.

"Mr Kennedy not around today?" Bates asked.

Shooting him a look, she replied, "No, not right now."

"Been a bit busy over the years, hasn't he, your old man?" McColl asked provocatively.

"Don't know what you mean by that, but I'm assuming you mean with work, so yes, things are going well with the business." Sandra smiled, reaching for the ashtray.

"He was inside for a while wasn't he?" McColl went on, "Must be nice to have him home again, imagine it must have been quite a lonely time for you?"

Sandra took another pull on her cigarette and exhaled, tapping her cigarette in the ash tray. "I was OK, I had family and friends around me, they looked out for me so I was OK, I was lucky." She smiled smugly.

"You have a lovely home," McColl observed.

"Thank you, Inspector. But I'm guessing the reason for your visit today is not to check out my interior." Sandra balanced the cigarette in the ashtray and placed the ashtray on the table. Smoothing down her cardigan, and biting back her irritation at having her afternoon interrupted, she spoke again, cutting the chase. "So, what's this about?"

"So your husband's in the building trade?" Bates asked. "Is that where he is now?"

Looking at Bates, Sandra replied, "Yes, he's gone to check out some new suppliers."

"That's good. Well, good for you, it means we won't be interrupted. Not sure how he would feel about us raking up the past so we'll try to keep this quick," McColl replied. "Have you seen much of Ken Allington recently?"

At the mention of Ken's name, Sandra froze. "No, why?" McColl let the question hang for a minute, observing and enjoying the reaction. "Well, I mean, he lives over the road to us but we never see Ken or have anything to do with him," Sandra added innocently.

"You were romantically involved at one point, weren't you? Don't you speak to each other anymore?"

Squirming uncomfortably, Sandra scowled and resumed smoking her cigarette. "Look, that was all a long time ago. I'd rather not discuss it if it's all the same to you. My husband is out now and has been for a while, I'd rather him not find out about what happened between me and Ken. It all in the past; besides, he's never really around so we don't ever see him anymore."

"You also knew Heidi Perthwaite, didn't you? Wasn't she going out with your son Kieran when she disappeared?" McColl asked.

"That's right, he was devastated when she ran off like that," Sandra said disapprovingly, shaking her head.

"Ran off? What makes you think she was a runaway?" Bates asked with interest.

"Well she was always a bit flighty, probably took up with someone else and took off," Sandra said flippantly.

McColl looked at Bates incredulously, and asked, "And who would Heidi have taken off with?"

"Oh I don't know, she had plenty of choice. Kieran could never keep up with the competition, she was a popular girl amongst the boys." Sandra shrugged dismissively. "She wasn't good enough for him anyway."

"You didn't approve of her?" McColl observed. Sandra shrugged and continued smoking her cigarette. Waiting for a response but not receiving one, McColl added accusingly, "But wasn't it Kieran who was cheating on Heidi?"

Sandra shrugged. "She drove him to it, always flirting with the other lads, what did she expect?"

Shocked at the cold response and attitude, McColl changed the subject slightly. "The night Heidi went missing, you saw Ken's car parked outside his house?"

"Think so, probably, yes," Sandra replied coolly.

"You think so?" Bates repeated, unable to hide his mounting irritation and dislike for the woman. "Well you either did or you didn't? She's been missing for nearly seven years, she was last seen that night and you're saying you can't be sure of what you saw that night?"

Rounding on Bates, Sandra snapped back, "Well it was a long time ago and I can't remember!"

Trying to diffuse the situation, McColl added calmly, "Sandra, we just want to be sure because you said in your statement that you saw Ken's car that night and it was parked across the street."

Taking a puff on her cigarette and stubbing it out, Sandra blew a puff of smoke up in the air and towards Bates' direction. "Well, I guess I did see Ken's car then," she added sarcastically.

"Did you visit your husband around that time?

Maybe Bob can remember you mentioning what you saw?" McColl asked innocently.

Clearly irritated and feeling backed into a corner, Sandra sighed and scooped her hair behind her ears. "Look, what do you want from me?" She appeared resigned and defeated. Slouching, Sandra shrugged her shoulders. "I've helped as much as I can, why are you here sniffing around again? Bob's kept his nose clean and I've told you all I know."

"Because I'm not sure I believe you, Sandra," McColl said. The room fell silent.

After a few minutes Bates tried a different approach. "Look Sandra, all we want is to get to the truth. This visit is off the record and anything you tell us now will go no further. We just need to find out if what you said to DCI Harold Spencer during your original interview was the truth. Maybe you could have held something back which you couldn't say at the time, we just want to be sure of the chronology of events that night."

Sandra stayed silent, and clasped her hands. She stared at her immaculate fingernails, thinking about what had just been said. Finally, after what seemed like an age, she spoke, hesitantly. "Spencer was killed in a car crash after what happened."

"Yes, that's right, he was moving to the Isle of Wight, looking forward to his retirement," Bates added.

"He came to see me, during the original investigation," Sandra began. "I told him what I know, I told him everything. There was a car parked outside Ken's house that night."

"OK," McColl said softly.

Sandra took a deep breath before adding, "…But it wasn't Ken's car, it was Harold's." Sandra sighed. DCI McColl and DI Bates stared at Sandra as she continued. "When DCI Spencer came to see me, I had said I had thought I saw Ken's car, but wasn't sure it was his."

McColl and Bates stared at each other; Bates eyes widened as he asked, "Harold's car was parked outside Ken's house that night? But why?"

"I don't know," Sandra replied, shaking her head. "I don't know, Harold said it must have been Ken's car, and I agreed, but I don't think it was. They were friends, you see. Sometimes I had seen Harold's car parked out on the pavement, whilst Ken's car was on the driveway. That night there was only one car on the driveway, and it wasn't Ken's."

"How comes this wasn't picked up before?" McColl asked.

"Probably because they were similar," Sandra conceded. "Harold Spencer was a copper, I wasn't about to go making trouble for myself and Bob, he was inside, anything could have happened to him. I had to protect him and protect Kieran." Sandra sighed. "Heidi had also found out I had been seeing Ken, I was worried she would go shooting her mouth off and Bob would find out. So when she disappeared, I didn't say anything."

McColl was reeling. Why was DCI Harold Spencer at Ken's house that night and where was Ken? Was he there, and if so where was his car that night?

"Will I need to tell Bob about me and Ken?" Sandra asked sadly.

"That's your choice, Mrs Kennedy," McColl replied, before adding coldly, "but secrets have a way of coming out. Thank you for your time, we'll see ourselves out."

They got up and left, as Sandra sat in a crumpled heap on the sofa, in the plush living room, in her comfortable surroundings. Suddenly aware that her existence in her ivory tower was all about to come crashing down.

Chapter 14

As they drove back to the station, McColl and Bates mulled over Sandra Kennedy's disclosure. "We need proof that it was Harold's car on Ken's drive that night," McColl thought aloud. "At the moment, all we have is Sandra's admission. Ken will say she's being malicious and it's because of their fall-out that she's saying all this."

Bates nodded as he drove along. "So what do we do, how can we prove it was Ken's car? Spencer's car was involved in that crash, we'll have to go through the old archives and get the details and registration number plate."

McColl nodded. "If Harold Spencer was a bent copper how do we know he was the only one?"

Bates went on, "And what was he up to? Do you think he was involved in the girl's disappearance?"

McColl shuddered and turned to look at Bates. "I don't know, but we are going to find out."

*

Friday evening came around and Marlon arrived at the Red Lion just after 7.30pm; he made his way through the crowded pub and found Kirsty sitting at a table by the window with her dad and her brother Matthew. "Hi, want a drink?" Marlon asked them.

Standing up to greet him, Kirsty smiled and hugged him. "Thanks for coming. We're good, thanks, Oliver's gone to the bar already. Marlon, this is my dad, John, and I think you've met Matt already?"

John stayed seated and stretched out his right hand, and gave Marlon's right hand a firm shake. "Hello son, how are you?" he greeted his daughter's friend with suspicion.

Feeling slightly uncomfortable, Marlon replied good-naturedly, "Yeah, I'm good thanks. Hi Matthew, I've seen you around campus, nice to see you again mate. I'm going to get a pint, sure you don't want one?"

Shaking his head, Matt smiled kindly and replied,

"No, I'm good thanks, Oliver's just getting a round in."

Marlon took his jacket off and put it on the back of one of the empty chairs on the opposite side of the table. He walked through the crowded bar and joined the queue. There was a lively, fun atmosphere, with lively banter and the air was thick with cigarette smoke and the smell of various aftershaves and perfumes. Turning away from the bar, Oliver had a tray of drinks in his hands. "Oh hi, you're Kirsty's brother aren't you, and it's Oliver right?"

Oliver didn't smile back, instead he responded coolly with, "That's right, and you're Marlon who wants to be my sister's boyfriend right?" Marlon was speechless, and unsure of how to react. "You take care of Kirsty, do you hear? Or you'll have me to answer to."

With that, Oliver walked off, plastered a big smile on his face and went back to the table. "Kirsty, this is yours, Christine and Kelly here's your drinks," he said, passing over two drinks to Kirsty's friends. "Dad, Matt, here's yours." Passing the drinks over, he lifted his pint glass and sipped at his lager.

"Oh, did you not get Marlon one? He was over at the bar with you," Kirsty said with disappointment.

"No, sorry, I had already been served by the time he'd arrived," Oliver said, feigning disappointment in response.

Sitting back down Oliver started chatting to Kirsty's friends. Kirsty got up. "Where are you going?" John asked.

"I'm just going over to help Marlon with the drinks while he's getting served." She walked over to the crowded bar and made her way through to where Marlon was standing. "Hiya, thanks for coming," Kirsty said, hugging him.

"That's OK, it's nice to be invited, and I don't think your brother likes me very much though." He laughed good-naturedly.

"Oh just ignore him, he's just a bit overprotective at times."

The bar maid came over and Marlon ordered a pint. "Did you want a drink?"

"OK then, I'll have a half," Kirsty replied.

They took their drinks back over and joined the rest of them at the table. Oliver frowned as they sat down. "Kirsty I already got you a drink," he said, scowling.

Kirsty smiled at her brother cheerfully in response. "It's OK, it won't go to waste." She turned to Marlon and they chatted amongst themselves, ignoring Oliver's beady eyes watching them. Oliver didn't like Marlon and wasn't about to make any secret of the fact that he disapproved of the relationship that was developing between Marlon and his sister. Marlon continued to ignore Oliver's attempts to make him feel uncomfortable but it was irritating him.

"So what subjects are you girls studying at college?" he asked, deflecting the attention and changing the subject.

John listened to the exchange, his gaze moving to the bar. Noticing someone familiar watching them, Matt followed his father's gaze. "Hey Dad, isn't that the police officer who came to see us about Molly?"

John put his pint down and strained his neck to see; sure enough, DCI McColl and DI Bates were over at the bar area, ordering drinks. "Oh yeah, you're right, they must be off their shift having a drink after work."

"Do you think they're watching us?" Matt asked.

Oliver shifted his attention to the bar area and sighed. "What are they doing here? Can't they leave us alone in peace for Kirsty's birthday?" John shot Oliver a look, warning him to calm down. Oliver picked up his pint and sipped at it, biting back his annoyance. John smiled at his son.

"Look, don't worry about them, let's just make sure Kirsty has a good night." They carried on talking about other things but Mathew had noticed the change in atmosphere and sensed there was more to this. Why was Oliver so bothered by the police being there and what was going on between his dad and his brother? Pushing his thoughts to the back of his mind, he laughed at something one of Kirsty's friends had said and tried not to dwell on it, but still felt slightly uneasy.

John went up to the bar after a while and acknowledged the police's presence. "Evening Inspectors, is this you off work or are we under surveillance?" he quipped light-heartedly.

McColl smiled and shook her head. "You've got me, we were just thinking you hadn't noticed us." Bates laughed and John smiled in amusement.

"Did you want to come over? You're welcome to join us? It's my daughter Kirsty's birthday, so we're just celebrating with a couple of her friends."

Bates' smile disappeared as he looked at McColl and waited to see what her response would be. "Yes John, what can I get you?" the bar man said before she could answer. John ordered some drinks and lifted the tray from the bar. McColl smiled and picked up her drink, threw her jacket over her arm and picked up her bag.

"Are you coming then?" McColl said as she followed John over to the table.

Bates grabbed McColl's arm. "What are you doing?" McColl shook Bates' hand off and replied innocently, "I'm having a drink after work, what does is look like? There's no harm in being social, besides, we might find out something."

Bates was stunned into silence and followed her over to the table where John, his sons, his daughter and her friends were sat. McColl took a seat next to John on the back sofa by the window. Bates took the other available stool next to Oliver. He nodded at Oliver as he sat down, picked up his pint and sipped at it. Oliver was not impressed and scowled in response. Sipping at his own pint he said, "So Inspectors, has there been any progress with your investigation into my sister's murder?"

DI Bates turned to Oliver and made eye contact as he replied, "We're looking into existing leads but no new ones have developed at this stage I'm afraid."

John looked sympathetically at DI Bates who was clearly uncomfortable at being put on the spot in front of everyone around the table. "Hey Oliver, tonight's about Kirsty, I'm sure the Inspectors will be letting us know as soon as there are any new developments that we need to know about."

McColl smiled at John and agreed, "Of course, Mr Symmonds, we really are doing all we can. However, if you do have any questions or if you need any updates, we will be happy to answer what we can." DCI McColl picked up her white wine and sipped it; changing the subject, she turned to Kirsty. "So I gather it's your birthday. Happy birthday. How old are you?"

Kirsty looked at McColl and smiled sheepishly, "I was seventeen the other day." Marlon watched how Kirsty blushed and felt a surge of emotion for her; Kirsty appeared to be so vulnerable at times. He really liked her and the more time Marlon spent with Kirsty and her family, the more he realised the loss of Molly had affected the whole family and Marlon didn't know what to say at times for fear of upsetting someone. Although Ryan had been adamant he had had nothing to do with what had happened to Molly, Marlon could not shake of his suspicions of him, although he had not said anything to Kirsty about it.

He and Ryan had been friends for a long time and Marlon felt guilty thinking badly of his friend.

Thinking about his conversation with Ryan, Marlon decided when he next saw Mark Turner he would ask him what he remembered about that night. If Ryan was in the other room at the party with Mark that night, then this would allay his fears. He listened to Kirsty as she chatted with her friends about college. "So, girls what subjects are you studying?"

One of the girls turned and replied, "We're both doing drama and sociology A-Levels." Her name was Christine and she was a pretty girl with a fun sense of humour.

"Yeah, we've been thinking about what we're going to do next when we leave college." the other girl called Kelly replied. "After we're finished maybe we could do a bit of acting work, there's a lot of money to be made in commercials from royalties."

Christine nodded in agreement. "Yeah, a couple of hours' work for a lifetime of royalties, I'll have some of that! I can buy myself a nice little convertible car." They laughed.

"Not that that's the only reason you girls are studying drama!" Kirsty chuckled.

"Here Kirsty, now you've passed your driving test you can think about getting one!" Kelly laughed conspiratorially.

"Yeah, well done sis, on passing your driving test yesterday. How are you enjoying your birthday drinks?" Matthew asked.

"Yeah, this is nice, I'm glad I agreed to this." Kirsty smiled happily.

"You deserve a good birthday," John replied smiling back at his daughter. "Everyone, I'd like to raise a toast to my wonderful, clever daughter, and your wonderful sister and friend Kirsty. May the year ahead be full of happiness, love and whatever your heart desires – except a convertible car!" John laughed.

"Cheers!" they all responded, laughing and raising their clinking glasses.

DCI McColl watched John as he fought back tears, seeing how hard this must be for him. It was unusual for her to join a bereaved family for drinks, although what she had said to Bates was true, she had wanted to see what she could find out; she also did not want to be unkind, and found herself drawn to John, and he was an interesting character. McColl wanted to find out more about him and could not shake the feeling that she was missing something. There was something that she could not quite put her finger on. Kirsty had previously made no secret of the fact that she did not trust Ken, and then there was the disappearance of the missing girl. McColl's head was swirling with recent events and she was determined to see what she could find out, however she was beginning to realise her own feelings were starting to make things more complicated.

Bates finished his drink and looked over at McColl; she shook her head. "I'm going to make a move I think," she said, picking up her jacket. "Thank you for having us," she said to John.

"I can drive you, I've only had the one," Bates said. McColl shook her head as she stood up and went to leave.

"No you're alright, stay if you want, pick the car up over the weekend."

Bates shook his head and went to join her. "No, it's fine, I want to get off anyway. I'll drop you home, Gov." As they said their goodbyes and left the pub, Oliver watched his father's reaction curiously. Was he disappointed? This surprised him because of his own relief he felt at the detective's exit.

Chapter 15

The following evening was Saturday night, as it was still early, Ken's bar wasn't busy. Ryan was sitting at the bar waiting for Ken serve him. A couple of young men had just been served and were making their way over to the jukebox. One decided to go on the fruit machine and the other went to put some tunes on. As some rock music blasted out Ken came over and pulled Ryan a pint. "So you seen anything of your friend Marlon lately?"

Ryan shook his head. "I tried calling him last night but couldn't reach him," he said, paying Ken for his pint. "I need you to do something about his friendship with that Kirsty, it's a bad idea." Ryan laughed.

"Oh really? Doubt it'll come to anything, Marlon

ain't that serious about her." He shrugged off the idea. Ken grimaced as he went to the till and was counting Ryan's change. "I don't want no more attention being drawn to this place. Since that other girl disappeared I don't want the old bill sniffing around here again." He went to give Ryan his change and saw Marlon approaching the bar behind Ryan. "Oh hi, what can I get you?"

Ryan looked around. "Oh, there you are. Where were you last night? I tried calling you."

"I'll get a pint please, Ken," Marlon replied. "Oh, did you? I was out," he replied to Ryan. Ken went to pull Marlon's pint, eavesdropping on their conversation. "Oh, I went to Kirsty's birthday drinks over at the Red Lion. Hey, what's up with him?" Marlon nodded in Ken's direction.

Ryan looked away. feigning boredom. "Oh, I don't know. So you were out with the Waltons last night?" he mocked Marlon.

"Hey, don't be like that," Marlon replied defensively, "they're alright as it goes, they're a nice family." Ryan grunted in response.

Ken came back and gave Marlon his pint. "£1.65, mate." Marlon counted Ken out the right money and picked up his pint.

"Oh that's nice, felt well rough earlier," he said, sipping at it.

"So what's going on between you two then? Are you two in a relationship now or what?" Ryan asked incredulously.

Marlon shrugged. "I don't know yet, it's too early to say, but... I like her." Marlon smiled to himself. His smile faded as he continued, "It's such a shame what happened to her sister Molly, man, that family have really been through it. I don't know how they're coping with it all to be honest."

Ryan looked at Ken. "Yeah, it's terrible."

Ken agreed. "Sure is. Poor Molly, there's some real arseholes out there." Ryan glared at Ken.

Ken walked off and Marlon pulled out a seat at the bar beside Ryan; he watched Ken, climbed up and looked sideways at his friend. "Seriously Ryan, what's going on between you and Ken? Have you two had some sort of a fall-out?"

Ryan said nothing but sipped at his pint, without looking up. Finally he looked up and met Marlon's gaze. "No. Look, I've already told you, I don't know what that guy's problem is, he probably just needs to get laid!" Ryan laughed at his own joke and shook his head, going back to his pint.

Marlon said nothing but continued watching him. He couldn't put his finger on it but knew his friend well enough to recognise Ryan was hiding something from him. Changing the subject, he looked around the bar. "Where is everyone tonight?"

Ryan shook his head. "Don't know, probably on their way. I haven't spoken to anyone today but know a few of the guys are coming down, Mark Turner texted me this morning."

Marlon nodded. "So how have you been, is Chloe coming tonight?"

Ryan gritted his teeth and replied, "I don't know," in a sarcastic sing-song voice. He was becoming weary of his friend's scrutiny and constant questions, and couldn't help snapping at Marlon. Catching sight of Marlon's hurt expression Ryan's face softened. "Hey, listen mate, I'm sorry, I've just had a lot on my plate lately. Chloe's been banging on about us moving in together again."

Marlon laughed. "You really need to put that girl out of her misery."

Ryan chuckled in response, the tension disappearing between them both. "I know, I'm a heart breaker. What can I say? The ladies can't get enough of me," he smiled.

The conversation turned to football and the usual politics that went with it. After an hour or so a group of their friends joined them. Marlon noticed Mark Turner was with them. "Hi mate, you alright?" Marlon smiled cheerily and gave Mark a high five that went into a bear hug.

"Yeah, I'm good mate, yourself?"

"Yeah, I'm cool, I ain't seen you in a while, what have you been up to?" Marlon asked, waiting for the right time to approach the subject about Christmas Eve.

"Just working, mate, you know how it is." He ordered some drinks and asked for some coins in the change for the fruit machine; Mark loved to gamble. He always made a point of saying he had got more out than he put in the machines but Marlon didn't believe this. Mark had a habit of overindulging in bad habits, and as a result his perception wasn't always accurate. Mark picked up his drink and headed over in the direction of the fruit machine. Casually, Marlon picked his own drink, and followed him.

Mark's face was alight with excitement and shone with the reflection of the lights from the fruit machine. He was like a kid in a sweet shop and his face was a picture of anticipation and joy as he was putting his first pound coin in. The machine whirred into action, and the wheels spun as the theme music played loudly. Two symbols came up, along with a number seven. Mark hit the 'hold' button underneath the seven; as he did so he shot Marlon a sideways look. "It's my lucky day, I can feel it!" he laughed. The wheels rolled and two different symbols appeared beside the seven. "Oh man," Mark grumbled under his breath. He hit the 'hold' button again, this time two more sevens rolled into the screen and stopped. "Yes!" Mark yelped excitedly. "Jackpot, baby, I knew it!"

As Mark was collecting his winnings, Ryan came over and joined them. "I think you'll find that's mine, mate." Ryan smiled with satisfaction. "You still owe me for the other week."

Mark's face was a picture of disappointment. "Oh, I thought I gave you that?" Mark's victory, quickly turned to defeat.

"Nope, you didn't, and don't try it." Ryan laughed wickedly. Mark's face fell, as he counted out £20 in coins and handed it over to Ryan. "Thanks mate, nice doing business with you," Ryan said cheerfully as he took the pound coins and disappeared again back over to the bar area to change the coins up into a note. Mark tutted and sighed with frustration. Taking another pound coin he went at the fruit machine again for another round.

With Ryan distracted and out of earshot, Marlon seized the moment. "Hey, so I don't think I've seen you properly since Christmas Eve."

Mark muttered to the machine under his breath, "Huh? Sorry? What was that?" he asked Marlon, clearly not hearing what he'd said. Marlon tried again.

"Christmas Eve, we were at that party, I didn't see you much there either."

Mark nodded in acknowledgement. "Oh yeah, I had to leave early, I promised I'd help my mum with something." Marlon nodded, staring at the fruit machine.

"Oh, so that's why I didn't see much of you," he continued carefully. "Yeah, I think we got there about 11.30pm."

Mark nodded. "Yeah, I left around midnight," he responded. "Was later than planned, my mum wasn't too happy about it." He chuckled with amusement. "But I did do what she asked me to, just later than planned."

Marlon laughed along, not quite sure where this

was all going. "Oh yeah? So what did you have to do?" he asked with genuine interest.

"My mum hid a bike up in the loft, I had to get it down and help wrap it after my little sister was in bed."

Marlon laughed and shook his head. "Bit dangerous when you've been drinking." He laughed with amusement.

"Yeah I know," Mark agreed. "Still, at least I didn't do any Charlie that night."

Marlon raised his eyebrows. "Didn't you? Ryan had some good stuff that night, we were wasted, man!" Mark nodded and gave the machine one last hit.

"I didn't see Ryan that night, we must've missed each other." Mark picked up his pint and sipped it, hitting the machine hard with his hand in frustration. "Oh man, I give up." He turned to look at his friend; Marlon was speechless and lost in his own thoughts. "Hey, you OK mate? You look like you've seen a ghost."

Marlon looked at his friend, "Huh? Oh yeah, sure, I'm fine." He gathered himself together quickly. "So you didn't see Ryan all night? I thought I saw you two catching up in the kitchen?"

"What? When?" Mark asked, confused. Marlon stared at Mark.

"Christmas Eve, that party we were at?" he pressed on.

Mark's face drew a blank. "Nope, sorry mate, must've been talking to somebody else, I told you, and I didn't see Ryan over Christmas until New Year."

Chapter 16

It was Monday morning in June, and DCI McColl was getting her morning coffee and toasted cheese sandwich in the police canteen. She carried her cup around to her office and sat down at her desk. Since looking into Molly Symmonds' murder, she had not been sleeping properly and would often find herself wide awake in the early hours, wondering if it was a one off or if the killer would strike again. Since Kirsty Symmonds' visit to the police station a couple of months before, it had started a chain of events. What if the young girl was right, and Ken was involved in what had happened to Molly? DCI McColl sighed as she rubbed her temples. She looked at the map on the wall. The park with the climbing frame, where Heidi had last been seen alive, was only half a mile from where Molly's body had been found, which was only yards from the Symmonds' family home. She noticed that Rosendale Avenue also fell within that half a mile; it couldn't all be a coincidence, could it? Heidi's home and Ken's home were also only a few roads away from each other, but were over two miles from where the other events had taken place.

She got up, eating her toasted cheese sandwich, and drew initials for people's names and locations of events on the map. She was so engrossed in her thoughts and drawings, DCI McColl didn't notice Bates appearing in the doorway behind her. "Morning Gov," DI Bates said, interrupting her thoughts. "You look busy there," he observed.

McColl turned, with her mouthful of sandwich, and put her hand up to cover her mouth as she spoke. "Morning, you alright?"

Bates nodded and came in, with his hands in his pockets. "What's all this then, Gov, you onto something?"

McColl took a sip of her coffee and washed down her food. "I'm not sure yet," she responded as she picked up her napkin and dapped her mouth.

"What time have you been in since?" he asked, perching on McColl's desk.

"Oh, not long, I got here just after 8.30am," she replied. "Look at this," she said, putting her cup down and going back over to the board. "Look where Ken's bar is," she noted. "It's right in the middle of where all these events have taken place." McColl marked a red X where Ken's bar was on the map.

Bates nodded. "What did you want to do, shall we bring him in?"

McColl thought for a moment, then she shook her head. "Not formally yet, but I do think we should pay him a little visit, see what he has to say for himself."

Bates grinned widely, and nodded with excitement. "Sounds good to me, boss."

*

The unmarked police car turned into Berringer Street just after 10am. DCI McColl pulled down her mirror in the car, put some lip gloss on and combed her hair. "Aye-aye, boss," Bates nodded, amused.

"Well, we know he likes the ladies." McColl grinned mischievously. "Let's see if I can work some of my charm on him."

They got out of the car and walked over to the front gate. They looked back over at Sandra's house with the high hedge. *If that hedge wasn't there, Ken would have been able to see right inside the living room window,* Bates thought to himself. They approached the front door slowly; as McColl had her hands in her blazer pockets, Bates leaned over and pressed the doorbell. They waited for a few minutes before Ken appeared in the doorway. He was dressed in grey tracksuit bottoms and a black T-shirt, clearly not expecting visitors. "Good morning Ken, mind if we pop in and ask you a few questions? It won't take long." McColl flashed a smile at him. Ken's face remained closed; he thought for a few seconds, then nodded.

"Sure, this is an unexpected pleasure." Ken smiled warmly as he opened the door and let the police officers through. McColl followed Ken through to the kitchen and made eye contact with Bates, who's face betrayed his curiosity as they followed Ken through the house.

Ken put the kettle on. "Tea or coffee?" he asked in a friendly chit-chat way.

"Oh, I'll have a tea please, two sugars," McColl replied.

Ken looked at DI Bates, who shook his head politely. "Not for me thanks, I've just had one," he lied.

Ken busied himself making the tea, as he asked curiously, "So, what's all this about then?" He put a tea bag in each cup and went over to the fridge to fetch the milk. As the kettle boiled, Ken put the milk down, and leaned against the side, putting his hands in his pockets, casually smiling.

McColl smiled back and responded, "We'd like to ask you about the night Heidi Perthwaite disappeared, and can you remember where you were? It was a Sunday, July 28th, 1990 to be precise." Ken frowned as though deep in thought, as the kettle hit the boil. He turned and poured the scalding water onto the tea bags, added the milk and stirred the cups.

"I think I already told your mate Harold Spencer all you boys in blue need to know – and girls in blue, of course." Ken chuckled at his own joke as he passed the cup to McColl.

McColl took the cup and noted Ken had forgotten to add the sugar. Saying nothing, she accepted the drink and said, "Thanks." Also noticing that Ken had not responded to the question, she pressed on, "So do you remember where you were, Ken?"

Ken smiled and replied, "As I told your mate Harold, I was here all evening." He smiled, blowing and sipping his tea.

McColl smiled. "How well did you know DCI Harold Spencer, Ken?"

Ken seemed surprised at the question. "What a question! Why'd you ask that?" He smiled with amusement.

Hiding her irritation, McColl replied, "No reason, please just answer the question, Ken."

Bates was not amused and his eagle eyes were studying Ken's reaction carefully. "We heard a rumour that his car was parked on your drive on Sunday 28th July 1990, now why would that be, Ken?" Bates added coldly.

Ken looked at them both, puzzled, and shook his head. "Nope, sorry but I don't know where you've been getting your information from, but somebody's been telling you porkies!" He chuckled. "Harold Spencer has never been to my house, so his car would never had been parked on my drive." He smiled. "Sure you didn't want a brew?" he asked Bates.

Bates didn't answer but watched Ken with irritation. Ken was clearly enjoying this little charade and Bates was struggling to hide his irritation. McColl sipped at her tea. "Oh Ken, I think you forgot to sugar this, do you mind?"

Ken looked over at McColl and took the cup. "Oh,

silly me, of course not, darling, give us it here." Ken smiled, as he took the cup and turned to add the sugar.

McColl made eye contact with Bates, warning him to let her take control. Ken turned back, stirring the cup of tea, and passed it back to McColl. She blew it and sipped it. "Thanks Ken," she said. "So you were here all evening?"

Ken nodded. "Yep, didn't go out and didn't do anything that night, had an early night," he said.

She smiled at him. "So you didn't answer how well you knew Harold Spencer, were you two friends?"

Ken's face darkened. "No. I've already told you, he only came once to ask questions during the door-to-door after that girl disappeared."

McColl tilted her head to one side thoughtfully. "So DCI Spencer did come to your house then?"

Ken looked at her, then shook his head. "Well he didn't come in if that's what you're getting at."

McColl smiled. "But his car would have been parked on your drive that day?"

Ken was ruffled and it was beginning to show. "Well yeah, but that would have been after that girl had disappeared!" he said defiantly. Aware of the sudden change in atmosphere, Ken turned and put his cup down. "Listen, I don't mean to be rude, but I've just remembered I've got to be somewhere. Is there anything else? Only I need to be getting on." Ken folded his arms, and leaned back against the side.

Enjoying taking back control, McColl smiled. "Oh just one more thing."

"Yes?" Ken sighed impatiently.

"You were involved with Sandra Kennedy around that time, weren't you?" Ken said nothing but looked at McColl with contempt. "I hear Bob's out now, must be nice for her having him around again. It's a shame things didn't work out between you two. We'll see ourselves out."

Chapter 17

A few weeks had gone by and Kirsty was at the library studying for some college homework. She had not heard from Marlon since her birthday. Although disappointed, she had put this down to Oliver's attitude towards Marlon at her birthday drinks. Kirsty made a mental note to catch up with Marlon at some point. Again she found herself drawn to the files on the missing girl. Heidi's Perthwaite's black and white picture was smiling back at her on the computer screen. She thought herself how old Heidi would be now possibly around twenty-four or twenty-five years of age. Her mind drifted to all the things Heidi could have been doing with her life, plus she was so lost in thought she didn't notice Marlon hesitantly approaching her from behind. He had a rucksack over his left shoulder and rubbed his chin as he came over gingerly.

"Kirsty?"

Kirsty shook her head as she abruptly came back to reality. "Oh hi." She blushed as she turned to face Marlon, embarrassed at being caught off guard.

"I thought it was you." Marlon smiled warmly. "How's it going?" he asked, looking over Kirsty's shoulder to see what she was engrossed in. Kirsty turned and looked at the computer screen guiltily.

"Yeah I'm OK, I was just researching something for my assignment." Marlon nodded, reading the headline on the screen with interest. 'Still No Links for Missing Local Girl'. Kirsty coughed nervously. "This wasn't actually for my assignment," she admitted with a grin. "I got distracted."

Marlon nodded, and grinned back, before saying seriously, "So is this the girl you think Ken knows something about?"

Kirsty didn't answer but said, "I can't believe the police never found any leads."

Marlon shook his head. "Listen, I'm sorry I didn't call you or get in touch for a while, I've just had a lot going on, and my uncle's store has been really busy. I don't know what it is with spring time, people just love a bit of DIY." Marlon laughed sheepishly. "Listen, I've got to get going, I'll see you around, don't get too distracted now." Marlon smiled as he pulled his rucksack higher over his shoulder and went to walk off.

Kirsty laughed. "I won't," she said, before adding quickly, "Hey, did you want to do something at the weekend, we could meet up?" Marlon stopped in his tracks and hesitated, but didn't answer straight away. Sensing Marlon's hesitation, Kirsty quickly backtracked, "It's OK if you're busy – some other time, hey?"

Marlon nodded, and swallowed, nodding, "Sure, some other time. I'll see you around."

Kirsty smiled, and turned back to the computer screen, but it stung. Why was Marlon turning cold on her? Was it Oliver or something else? Swallowing down her humiliation, Kirsty turned her attention back to her college research. But the feeling of hurt stayed with Kirsty long after Marlon had left her in the library.

Chapter 18

It was Saturday morning in July and Oliver was lying on the sofa watching Match of the Day. The football highlights were on TV and he clicked the volume on the remote control as his attention was captured by the latest result, showing on the screen. Oliver lit a cigarette and was enjoying his smoke when the doorbell rang. Tutting to himself but not moving, he waited to see if anybody else was around who would answer the door. The thought then occurred to him that it might be Karen ringing the doorbell. Oliver jumped up, and smoothed his T-shirt down. He made his way out to the mirror on the wall in the hallway and checked his reflection briefly. Oliver opened the front door; to his surprise and disappointment he found DCI McColl with DI Bates at her side.

"Morning, it's Oliver isn't it?" McColl asked. "Glad we caught you indoors, think we keep missing you." McColl smiled. "Is now a good time to have a little catch up?"

Oliver shrugged, responding, "Sure, why not?" Oliver walked back into the house; they followed him into the living room. He sat back down on the sofa he had been lying on before he was disturbed. Picking up the ashtray, he went back to his cigarette. Oliver waved his free hand at the other sofa and said, "Sit down, if you like." Bates stayed standing by the living room door, and took out a small note pad and his pen. He flipped over the top page as McColl took a seat on the other sofa, adjacent to Oliver's.

"We wanted to ask you about when you used to work at Ken's bar," DCI McColl began.

Oliver nodded, as he took a puff on his cigarette. "Oh yeah?" he asked with curiosity. "What about it?"

McColl clasped her hands and continued. "Do you remember the day when a young local girl disappeared, her name was Heidi Perthwaite?"

Oliver nodded. "Vaguely, yes."

McColl pressed on. "Were you working that day?"

Oliver nodded. "Yeah, I was, I finished at 4 o'clock."

"Oh, you sound pretty certain." McColl was surprised at his accuracy with the time, given how many years ago it would have been. Oliver shrugged and nodded, continuing his smoke. He picked up the remote control and reduced the volume on the TV.

"Yeah, I'd been late a few times so I had a row with Ken that day, he fired me," he added.

McColl looked up at Bates who was taking all this down. "Really? What happened?" McColl pressed on.

Oliver shook his head and shrugged again. "Just that, I was sick and tired of Ken's constant sniping at me and nagging, I'd had enough so I told him to do one, and he sacked me." Oliver finished his cigarette, and stubbed it out in the ashtray.

McColl frowned. "Did he not give you any warning?" she asked.

Oliver shook his head. "No." Then added sarcastically, "Plus he did love to show off in front of his mates, and I wasn't having it anymore." McColl nodded, listening with genuine interest.

"Did he used to do that a lot then in the bar?"

Oliver nodded, clearly still irritated. "Yeah, especially when one of them was a copper."

McColl's heart skipped a beat, and she gasped.

"Which copper?" Before Oliver even answered she knew the response he would give. Oliver shook his head as he tried to remember.

"Think his name was Spencer."

*

Marlon was in the hardware store; the day had been a typically busy one for a Saturday and he was looking forward to finishing for the day. Most Saturdays Marlon would meet up with Ryan and the boys for a few beers, however, since the last time Marlon had seen Ryan he had kept his distance. Pushing the till closed as he gave his last customer their change, Marlon ripped their receipt from the till and handed it to them with their change. "Thanks, have a nice evening." Marlon smiled as they left the hardware store with their goods. Walking over to the door to the shop behind the customers as they left, Marlon locked the door from the inside and turned the sign over to 'Closed'. As he did so, his mobile buzzed in his back pocket as a text message was received. Marlon took his mobile out of his back pocket from his jeans and read the message: 'Ken's bar 8pm be there or be square.' It was from Ryan. Marlon closed the message and put his phone back into his back pocket. Frank came around from the back of the shop and noticed Marlon's reaction to the text message. "Everything OK, Marlon?" Frank asked his nephew.

Marlon looked up at Frank. "Yeah, I'm fine." He smiled sadly. Marlon walked past the shelves, behind the counter and pulled the door closed as he took his navy blue apron off and hung it up on the hooks on the back of the door. Frank studied his nephew carefully and guessed it was girl trouble which was getting Marlon down. Frank also took his apron off, and hung it up beside Marlon's.

"Do you know, when I was your age, things were a lot simpler back then. These mobile phones make you too dependent on text messages. Things are generally much better when you're speaking to someone face to face, and talk more rather than texting." Marlon smiled, and picked up his jacket. Frank looked at his nephew sadly. "What's wrong, Marlon? I can tell something's wrong, what is it? What's bothering you?" He patted his nephew's shoulder in a gesture of comfort.

Marlon smiled and became defensive again. "Nothing, I'm fine, seriously, so you can stop with the fussing," he chuckled dismissively.

Frank, however, wasn't buying it. "Is this about your mystery girl?" he teased affectionately. Marlon grinned sheepishly, but didn't answer. Frank pressed on. "So, who is she then?"

Marlon sighed, thinking, it wasn't going to go anywhere anyway so he might as well tell him. "Kirsty Symmonds." Frank's smile faded. "What is it? You seem surprised." Marlon asked.

Frank put his jacket on as he absorbed this new information. "That's the girl who's sister was murdered isn't it?" Marlon nodded. "I thought you were suspicious of Ryan's movements that night?" Marlon nodded.

"Yeah, I was..." He stopped himself from continuing.

There was an awkward silence which hung in the air. Frank waited for Marlon to defend Ryan, and to say his concerns were unfounded, but it didn't happen. "Does she know?"

Marlon shook his head. "I didn't know how to tell her, and I wasn't sure so I didn't say anything. I didn't want to cause trouble. Besides, I've stopped seeing her now." Frank said nothing but gathered his belongings together. He made his way to the door of the shop; Marlon stared after his uncle with curiosity.

Frank glanced back briefly. "What?"

Marlon looked at his uncle. "Nothing, I'm just surprised that you're not encouraging me to fight for her and to work things out."

Frank shook his head. "It's none of my business. That Ryan though, he's bad news, I've told you that before. You keep that girl away from him, do you hear?" Marlon raised his eyebrows in surprise. "You think I don't know what you boys get up to when you're around Ryan? That boy is bad news."

Chapter 19

It was coming up to the August bank holiday weekend at the end of the month. John was at home, sorting out some laundry while the house was quiet. As he was doing so, he found a cardigan in the pile of clean washing which belonged to Molly. He stopped as he came across the soft material and lifted it slowly out of the basket; John held it to his face and gasped as he fought to hold back the tears. The pain was still so raw, that when memories of his daughter hit him the pain was like a knife through his heart. John wondered if the pain would ever fade, not that he would ever want it to, he thought to himself. Since he had seen the police officers at the Red Lion at Kirsty's birthday drinks, he hadn't heard anything from them. He just couldn't understand who would do something like this to his daughter; what kind of monster must they be. John grimaced as he put the garment down. He walked out into the hallway, grabbed his car keys, picked up his jacket, and left the house.

*

DCI McColl was sat at her desk; she was going through the Heidi Perthwaite file. The file was old and dusty and had been neglected for years. She was trying to establish whether there was a way of linking events together. The Narcotics Team had been working on the double shootings case and the powers that be had determined that the shootings were related to an organised gang who dealt in cocaine. McColl got up from her desk, and walked over to the board with the notes on from her own investigation. The flats where the shootings took place were already linked to a successful raid which had taken place before the shootings had happened. The raid had taken place a few months before and as a consequence of the substantial gains from the raid, and the money involved in the operation, the shootings had been kept strictly with Narcotics. McColl looked at the photo of Alexandra Sullivan. Something just did not sit right with her. The girl just did not look like the typical sort of girl who would get mixed up in drugs. The boyfriend, Sam

Osborne, possibly, he had had a swagger about him, plus he was friends with Ryan Reynolds who the police had long suspected of dealing but had no proof. The kid never had anything on him. Somebody must have been helping him, but who, McColl wondered to herself.

Ryan's rumoured girlfriend Chloe was also friends with Maxine, who lived in the flats. Alexandra had been going to see Maxine and Chloe on the night of the shootings. Alexandra never made it out of the car, and Chloe ended up not going at the last minute. Just as well, McColl though to herself, Chloe could have been shot as well, or instead. Suddenly McColl stopped. She shook her head and then went over to her door and stuck her head out to call Bates. As she did so, she noticed a familiar face waiting at the reception desk. Walking over, she smoothed her top down. "Mr Symmonds, how can I help?"

"Please, just call me John." He smiled nervously, then stammered, "At Kirsty's birthday drinks you said I could pop in for an update anytime. I wondered how the investigation was going."

McColl smiled and said, "Of course, come on through," She pressed the buzzer inside the door, and opened it for John to come through. McColl led the way through the back office, and into the corridor. They walked past a few rooms, until they reached one with the door open. McColl switched the sign on the door to say 'Occupied' and went through. John came in behind her; she shut the door, and went over to the green chairs. John sat down beside her. "So, how have you been doing, John?"

He smiled sadly. "Just taking things day by day, you know?" McColl nodded. "So what's the latest, have you got any new leads?" His voice was hopeful, but not expectant. McColl shook her head sadly.

"No new leads I'm afraid, and the ones we were exploring never ended up taking us anywhere." She waited before continuing. "John, do you have any idea who might have been following your daughter? Did Molly ever mention anyone to you, maybe a boyfriend she might have fallen out with?" John shook his head.

"No, Molly wasn't seeing anyone, she was a sensible girl, always concentrating on her studies."

McColl listened with interest, "Well, how about someone who might have been interested in her? Do you know if anyone wanted to get to know her better, perhaps had designs on getting intimate with her? The crime scene indicates that the perpetrator was somebody who may have been rejected by Molly, somebody who didn't take kindly to being rejected."

John thought for a moment. Thinking back to the conversation he had with Doreen a few months back he added slowly, "Look, I don't know if this could be something useful, it's probably nothing, but I was in the café on the high street a few months ago."

McColl listened carefully with interest. "Which one?" John rubbed his chin and sat forward, clasping his hands.

"I think the woman's name is Doreen who runs it." McColl nodded, acknowledging she understood where he meant. "Well, the lady that runs it – Doreen – she did mention that someone called Ryan had taken an interest in Molly."

"Oh really?" McColl took out her notepad and took this down.

"Yeah, I didn't know who she was on about though," John added honestly. "I think she said she'd heard a group of the college lads chatting."

McColl put her notepad away. "OK, well, thanks for letting me know, John, I'll get someone to look into it." John nodded, but said nothing. "If you think of anything else, do pop in again and let us know."

John nodded. "Sure, will do." He got up and walked over to the door. "Thank you for seeing me," he said, touching her arm as she opened the door. McColl looked up and smiled kindly in response; her heart lurched in her chest as she did so.

*

After John had left, McColl went to see her superior. The new information made no difference, it was clear the Narcotics Team's investigation was heading towards its climax and with a dawn raid planned in a few weeks, nothing could be done to jeopardise the expected results. It all hung on an informant giving the tip-off. However, the tip-off never came, and the raid never happened. McColl became increasingly frustrated as she could see a clear link between the shootings, Ryan Reynolds and Molly Symmonds. However, without questioning Ryan, there was nowhere for her investigation to go.

*

Matthew was at home, reading up on his coursework; his mind wandered to his twenty-first birthday, which was only in a few days' time in September. He had agreed to a party and his dad had busied himself over the last few weeks putting arrangements together; he had even said he had got himself a date for the party.

Matthew shook his head, as he thought of them together. Dad's mystery woman had certainly put a smile back on his face, he had been seeing her for a few weeks but none of the family had met her so there was some added excitement for his birthday party. It was due to take place in a hall on the campus by his college. There would be a few familiar faces there, as well as some new ones from a nearby campus. Matthew smiled a genuine smile for the first time in what had felt like a long time.

Kirsty came home from college; she hung her bag on the banister at the bottom of the staircase, and hung her jean jacket over it. "It's a scorcher today, I didn't need that jacket," she said, smiling as she walked into the kitchen. Looking over at her brother who was engrossed in his books she asked, "What you up to?" as she poured herself some juice from the fridge.

Matthew looked up briefly. "Oh, I'm just finishing this assignment, it's due in on Monday," he said. Kirsty nodded.

"Still reading up on American presidents?" she asked with interest.

Matthew chuckled and nodded. "Yeah, keeps me out of mischief!" Kirsty rinsed her glass in the sink.

"There's a lot of work involved in your course, are you still enjoying it?" she asked.

Matthew nodded again. "Yeah, I really am as it goes. I've been thinking about what I want to do after the course finishes. I'm thinking of applying for the student exchange programme to go to the States, see what it's like."

Kirsty was surprised. "Really? Wow, aren't you a bit too old to be an exchange student?"

Matthew stopped reading briefly. Looking up, he smiled. "No, there's a specialised work-study program that's available for older students. My tutor was telling us about it a couple of days ago."

Kirsty smiled, and raised her eyebrows but said nothing. She couldn't help but wonder how their dad would react to this and was concerned he might be still too fragile to cope with Matt leaving and going so far. "Have you discussed this with Dad?" she asked with interest. Matthew shook his head.

"No; I figured I'd wait until he's in a good mood." He smiled, then went back to his work.

Kirsty nodded and smiled, before adding, "Do you know, he does seem quite chipper lately, since he's been dating again. Do you know who she is?"

Matthew shook his head without looking up, and replied, "No, why hasn't he said anything to you about her? Being a woman and all, I would have thought he would have at least told you something about her."

Kirsty laughed wryly and shook her head. "No, he hasn't told me anything about her, I don't even know her name."

Chapter 20

Matthew's twenty-first birthday fell on a Saturday so the party was due to take place on the evening of the 6th September 1997. The hall had been decorated during the daytime by Kirsty, Oliver and a couple of their friends. They had all pitched in for the decorations so had quite a bit of preparing to do that day, and with the four of them it had only taken a couple of hours. The hall looked lovely, John thought, as he came in that evening with the cake. John was carrying it across to the tables by where the food was. The caterers were some old friends of Elaine's; they had put on a nice spread as a gift so it had not cost them anything. As John went to put the cake down, he saw Kirsty approaching out of the corner of his eye. John had been expecting this so he was prepared to fob her off and avoid her questions about his date. "Hi Dad, the food looks great doesn't it? The cake looks lovely, can I help with anything?" she asked, glancing at the cake.

"Erm, yeah, as it goes; there's some more cutlery in the car, can you go and grab it?" he asked, holding out the car keys to Kirsty, knowing this would shut the conversation down.

Surprised by the quick response, she replied, "OK, sure," and took the keys from her dad. Before she could say anything else, John walked off to the gents' toilets. Kirsty sighed loudly and rolled her eyes; she walked out to the car park to fetch the cutlery. Looking over his shoulder, as the door to the gents' closed John took his phone out of his pocket. Going over to the urinals he sent a text message, "Let me know when you're here x," and put his phone back in his pocket.

*

About an hour after the party had started, Marlon arrived with Ryan. They walked over to the bar; Ryan swaggered behind Marlon, looking around him as they arrived. "So who's party is this anyway?" Ryan asked as he took in his surroundings. His eyes wandered after a group of girls heading into the ladies' toilets by the entrance to the hall. One of the girls had glanced over and smiled as they disappeared from his view as the door closed behind them.

"It's Matt's twenty-first, you know that guy from the uni campus. Mark's mates are coming, it should be a laugh," Marlon replied. He hadn't mentioned to Ryan that Matthew was Kirsty's brother.

"Hey boys, mine's a pint if you're getting them in," Mark said, grinning widely. He greeted them both, a high five into a bear hug.

"Sure, I'll get them in." Marlon signalled to the bar tender as he waited to be served. Ryan and Mark walked across the hall to join some friends, they were checking out the girls that were there and eyeing up what talent there was, as Ryan caught sight of Kirsty and grimaced.

"What's she doing here?"

Mark looked over to where Ryan's attention was. "Who?" he asked, straining to see. "Oh, that's Kirsty, Matt's little sister." Ryan was stunned as he realised who's party they were at. Before he could say anything, Matt came over and joined in the conversation. Marlon came over and joined them with three pints. He handed one to Ryan, one to Mark and gave the other to Marlon.

"Happy birthday mate, thanks for the invite. Here, take my pint, I'll get another one."

Matthew was touched by the generosity. "You sure? Thanks mate."

"No worries." Marlon smiled. "So, great party mate, you got many people coming?" They chatted for a few minutes.

Kirsty had been sitting at one of the tables to the side of them. She got up and walked over to the bar and ordered herself a drink. "Can I get a double vodka and Coke please?" As she waited for her change, she took a big gulp of the sweet alcohol in an attempt to swallow down her anger. *What the hell is he doing here?* she thought to herself. As she turned to return to her seat, she came face to face with Marlon who had returned to the bar to buy another pint.

"Hi Kirsty," Marlon said sheepishly.

"Hi," she replied, and walked past him, returning to her seat. Marlon walked over to the bar, and waited to be served. His ego had been dented by the abrupt brush off, but he hid his hurt reaction and waited patiently for his pint.

Kirsty's heart was racing as she returned to her seat, but she would be damned before she set herself up for another rejection. The encounter at the library still stung, and she was not in a hurry to feel that way again. As she rejoined Oliver she noticed her father walking over to the entrance to the hall. John smiled as he held open the door and greeted his companion. Both Oliver and Kirsty's jaws fell open and their eyes widened in complete surprise as in walked DCI Sally McColl.

*

The party went well, both Kirsty and Oliver had been polite and civil to Sally McColl, although neither could quite believe their dad had been hooking up with a police officer, and a DCI at that. Matthew had hardly noticed as he had been busy catching up with his friends and receiving birthday gifts all evening. Towards the end of the party, McColl came over to the table and picked up her jacket from the back of one of the chairs by where Kirsty was sitting. "Nice seeing you, Kirsty, I need to go, early start tomorrow."

Kirsty smiled. "Yeah, thanks for coming."

McColl hesitated before saying, "I think there might be someone who wants to talk to you," she said, nodding back over her shoulder. Kirsty looked around McColl to see Marlon standing awkwardly at a distance. "Give him a chance, see what he's got to say for himself." McColl smiled, as she picked up her bag.

"See you later," she said as she walked away.

Marlon approached the table slowly. As he sat down he said, "Please Kirsty, don't leave," as Kirsty stood up to go.

"Why?" she asked curtly. "There's nothing to say." Marlon's face crumpled.

"Please, can we talk, just for a minute?"

Kirsty frowned, and sat back down, folding her arms. "Make it quick, I want to go home. Besides, I thought you'd made your feelings pretty clear last time we saw each other." Marlon was hurt and it showed. With the combination of alcohol and emotion, he lunged forwards to kiss her, but Kirsty pushed him away. "Marlon, get off." She sighed.

Ryan, seeing the scene unfolding couldn't resist coming over, laughing as he did so. "Take that shame, hahahaha. Oh come on, mate, she ain't worth it. She's just a frigid bitch anyway."

Marlon stood up and spun around; before Ryan could react, Marlon's fist swung through the air and landed on the left side of Ryan's cheekbone. The full force of the blow sent Ryan flying backwards, losing his balance, he landed on the dance floor behind him.

McColl, who was coming out of the ladies' at that

moment, rushed over and came in between the men before the situation escalated. "OK guys, that's enough, let's break it up. You OK?" she asked as she helped Ryan to his feet. His nose was beginning to stream with blood. She pulled her silk scarf away from her neck and wiped up the blood from Ryan's face, and held his arm to support him, but Ryan shook her off.

Wiping a hand across his face, he looked at the blood and laughed, shaking his head. "Nice. Didn't think you had it in you," he laughed nastily.

"Go home, Ryan," Marlon growled. "And take your opinions with you." Kirsty was shocked, she had never seen Marlon so angry. Ryan laughed, a dry sarcastic laugh; he looked at Kirsty then back at Marlon. "I'll allow you that one," he scoffed, before adding, "but next time I'll be coming for you." With that, Ryan turned and swaggered away.

*

The next day McColl arrived for work just after 10am; it was a Sunday, and she had some paperwork to catch up on whilst it was quiet, before the new week started. As she hung her coat up on the hook, she felt something in her pocket. Putting her hand inside she felt the cold material and pulled it out to see what it was. She pulled out her scarf from the night before and tutted to herself, realising she had forgotten to put it in the washing basket. She had been drinking at the party and had been so tired by the time she had arrived home she had dumped her coat on the end of her banister and gone straight to bed. She stuffed the scarf back in her pocket, mentally scolding herself for leaving it in there overnight. The smell would be awful to get out, as would the stain, she thought to herself.

McColl went over to her desk and sat down; she pulled out the files and started flicking through one, and it was her off-the-record file notes from the Narcotics investigation. Here and there she had been jotting down what information she could, in the hope something might tie up to her investigation. There was still no link to Ryan Reynolds from the Narcotics Team's investigation so far from what she could gather. He was definitely on something at the party the evening before, she thought to herself, probably cocaine; but how would she prove it? Feeling frustrated at not being able to arrange for an arrest to take place she picked up her pen and rubbed it along the end of her nose, moving the pen up and down sideways. *Surely there must be some way…* she thought to herself. Then her heart skipped a beat as she gasped. Suddenly she stopped breathing and her hands came down onto her desk. McColl turned slowly, and she looked back over at her coat, which was still hanging on the coat stand behind the door. Taking a deep breath, she pushed her chair back away from her desk and pulled herself up to standing, leaning on her desk. McColl stared at her coat for what seemed like an eternity, before slowly, she walked across her office and put her hand back in her coat pocket.

Slowly, she pulled the scarf out of her pocket; the material felt cold between her fingers, and it dropped effortlessly into her hand. She opened the scarf up and stared at the bloodstain from the night before. Sure enough, Ryan's blood was still there. Her mind was racing. The National DNA Database had only been set up two years ago. Although it was still in its early stages, data had started being collected from crime scenes and was being added onto the database. Although data for offenders who were not formally charged or were found not guilty was deleted, where charges had been brought against someone there was a chance the information was on the database for crimes which had occurred within the past two years. Even if Ryan had not been charged for something, if he had been involved in something and the Narcotics Team had a trace of Ryan's DNA it would be on the database. McColl wondered whether the team would be interested in running a sample of Ryan's DNA to see if there was a match, linking him to their investigation. For charges to be brought against Ryan, the DNA swab would need to be taken with Ryan's consent, but she was sure there would be a way for them to figure that out, especially with the amount of money and resources that was being poured into their investigation, she thought to herself cunningly.

Chapter 21

A few days later, Kirsty agreed to meet up with Marlon. They met in the café again and Marlon was waiting in a seat at a table over by the window. "Hi." He stood up and smiled nervously.

"Hi," she replied, sitting down opposite him.

"Thanks for coming. How are you?" Marlon asked. Doreen came over as they made themselves comfortable. "I'll get a coffee please, did you want one?"

Kirsty shook her head. "No thanks, I can't stay long. I need to be somewhere," she said.

Marlon's face crumpled. Although Kirsty had appreciated Marlon's loyalty and defending her honour at the party, she couldn't shake the feeling of rejection, being swept aside, and forgotten about for months. As far as she was concerned, the damage had been done, and Kirsty was not about to get involved with someone who was blowing hot and cold with her, she just wanted to concentrate on her studies.

"I'm sorry Marlon, but I think it's best if we stay just friends." Kirsty sighed as she saw his face fall. Marlon was heartbroken but he understood where Kirsty was coming from.

Putting on a brave face, he looked up into her eyes and said, "OK, that's cool." He forced a smile. "Maybe we could still hang out sometime?"

Kirsty smiled briefly and responded with, "Maybe, we'll see," being non-committal.

Changing the subject, Marlon asked, "So did your brother enjoy his birthday?"

Relaxing at the change in subject, she replied, "Yeah he did, everyone had a great time."

Marlon laughed. "I saw your dad enjoying himself, how long has he been dating that copper for?" She laughed and smiled.

"Yeah, my dad seems really happy lately, we didn't even know who he was seeing until she showed up Matt's birthday." Her smile faded when she added, "There hasn't really been anyone since our mum died." Marlon's coffee arrived and thanked the waitress, taking the cup from her.

"What happened to your mum – if you don't mind me asking?" he asked, tentatively. Kirsty shook her head.

"No, it's OK, I like talking about my mum. My family don't really talk about her, guess with men it's different. Me and my nan used to always talk about Mum with my sister Molly. Then after Nan died it was just me and Molly. Now it's just me," Kirsty said sadly, looking down at the table. Marlon sipped his coffee and said nothing, he waited to let her finish, sensing Kirsty needed to talk. "It was cancer. My mum passed away in 1986."

Marlon put his cup down and put his hand on hers. "I'm sorry to hear that."

Pulling her hand away, she looked back up at him, continuing, "My mum grew up in Edenbridge, there's a little town there and that's where she grew up before moving to around here. That's how she knew Ken, they grew up there together. When my mum moved here for college, that's how she met my dad, it was in the 70s. They fell in love, got married, had kids, and settled down here."

Marlon listened with interest. He cocked his head

to one side and asked, "So how comes Ken moved down here? Were they seeing each other - your mum and Ken?"

Kirsty burst out laughing. "What? No way! My mum had way better taste than that!" Marlon laughed and shook his head, raising his eyebrows. "I think he did have designs on my mum though," she added. "He moved down here after my mum did. Then when his uncle died, he inherited the land back in Edenbridge. He sold it and bought the bar, think he wanted to impress my mum. It didn't work though." She laughed, rolling her eyes. Marlon laughed as well.

"My Uncle Frank knows Ken, he's known him for years, and apparently Ken still goes out to Edenbridge quite regularly. He must still have family out there."

Kirsty looked puzzled, and shook her head. "No, that can't be right, Ken doesn't have any family. His mum walked out on his dad when he was young, and his dad died in a farming accident when Ken was a teenager. That's how his uncle ended up running the farm." Marlon was surprised.

"Oh, I didn't know, wonder what he gets up to in his spare time then."

Kirsty shook her head and said honestly, "As far as I'm aware Ken has no family left." She frowned and said, "I've never trusted that man. Sometimes I'd catch him looking at me and my sister when we were growing up, and I don't know, something wasn't right about the way he looked at us. He made me feel uncomfortable. Molly could never see it though." Marlon listened with interest.

"Do you still think he had something to do with what happened to your sister?"

Kirsty frowned and said, "I don't know," she looked out of the window again, "but one thing I do know is that I would never put anything past that man."

*

It was a cold November day when Matthew heard back about the Student Exchange Programme. "I'll be leaving after Christmas, most likely in January."

John choked back his tears and hugged his son to him. "I'm proud of you, son," John said with a lump in his throat.

Matthew looked at his dad and said with concern, "Dad, if you don't want me to go then I'll decline the offer."

John patted his son on the back and said firmly, "No. This family needs to find a way of moving on with our lives, I want you to go for it."

Matthew nodded before saying, "If you want me to stay, I'll stay." But John wasn't having any of it.

"It's what Molly would have wanted."

Christmas came and went, and before he knew it, John was driving to the airport. Kirsty and Oliver came to see their brother go. "I'll be back in October, it's only ten months!" Matthew laughed as he hugged them at the departure gates.

John looked at his remaining two children and put an arm around each of them. "I'm so proud of your brother, he's moving forwards with his life. It's time we all did the same."

Chapter 22

Marlon was working in his Uncle Frank's store. It was a Saturday in late January in 1998 and Frank was singing along badly to a tune, Six by Mansun, on the radio. Marlon chuckled to himself. "Hey, it's nice to hear you laughing for a change!" Frank smiled cheerfully. Marlon smiled.

"You back on with that girl?" Frank asked. Marlon shook his head sadly.

"No, we're just going to be friends," he said, "but it's cool, we still text and chat and stuff." Marlon carried on moving some boxes around in the shop. He came around to the back. "Hey Frank?"

"Yeah?" Frank responded, putting his pen behind his ear and coming over.

"How well do you know Ken Allington?" Marlon asked.

Frank frowned and scratched his chin, a look of consternation on his face. "Ken from the bar? Why?"

Marlon continued without answering. "Did you know he owned some land back in Edenbridge a few years back?"

Frank nodded. "Yeah, still does as far as I'm aware, why'd you ask?" Marlon frowned.

"I thought he sold it a few years back?"

Frank thought for a moment. "Erm, no, well, he did sell some of it, but he did keep part of it, it's where he grows his food produce for the bar, why the sudden interest?"

Marlon was surprised. "Oh, just wondered, that's all. Are you sure he still owns some land there?" Frank nodded.

"Yeah, I'm sure of it, I think he used to own some cattle there as well, not sure if he still does."

Marlon nodded but was distracted. "Oh right, is that why he drives out there regularly?"

Frank nodded. "I think so," before continuing. "Marlon, Ken's fingers dabble in a lot of pies, if you want my advice you'll stay out of his affairs."

Marlon didn't reply. Instead he continued unpacking the boxes of supplies and began refilling the shelves in the shop. His mind started wandering back to when he and Ryan were growing up. They had a lot in common as youngsters. With Ryan's dad working away a lot on business, Ryan was left in the sole care of his mother. She was a materialistic woman who spent much of her time over the years frittering away her husband's rather generous salary. As a young child, Ryan was passed from the care of one nanny to another. Ken had stepped in as a father figure during Ryan's teenage years, and Ryan had spent a lot of time hanging out at Ken's house, not that either of his parents would have noticed. That was when Ryan had stated taking cocaine and had introduced Marlon to it when they were teenagers. Although Marlon had dabbled on a few occasions, he had never let it consume him. As Ryan had become more and more involved in the murky, addictive world of drugs, Marlon had noticed his friend's personality changing over the years. Ryan was no longer the innocent kid he had known, loved and grown up with, Ryan had changed. Although Marlon's dad had left his mum when he was growing up, Frank had been like a father figure to him. Frank's sister had been heartbroken when Marlon's dad had left, but with his father's temper and quick fists, it wasn't a great loss when he did eventually walk out on them. Growing up, Ryan had been like a brother to Marlon, but now with his feelings towards Kirsty becoming clear to him, Marlon was realising his friendship with Ryan was coming to an end.

"Are you OK Marlon?" Frank's voice interrupted his thoughts. Marlon shook his head, startled, coming back to reality.

"Yeah, I'm fine," Marlon replied. "Whereabouts did you say Ken still had land?"

Frank put his pen back behind his ear and scratched his head. "Well, there used to be an old barn about two miles off from the main road, there's an allotment beside it just a few feet away, I think that's the part he still owns. He has a friend out there who helps with harvesting and keeps the place running for him." Frank went to walk off then stopped. Turning, he asked his nephew, "Why do you ask, Marlon? I don't know what you're thinking but I hope you're not planning on going out there, Ken won't thank you for interfering with his business," Frank warned him.

"Don't be silly, of course I'm not," Marlon laughed. The door opened and a customer came in and approached the counter.

Frank did not lose eye contact with Marlon until he spoke to the customer. "Yes sir, how can I help you?"

*

McColl was out on her lunch break when her mobile went. She pulled the Motorola handset out of her pocket with one hand as she accepted her change with the other. "Thank you," she mouthed at the cashier, leaving the fast food restaurant with her brown bag; she stuck it under her arm as she answered the call. "McColl," she said as her standard response to the caller. "Yes, yes, OK, really? Well how long will that take?" It was Forensics; the Narcotics Team were interested in running the DNA sample to see if it matched anything on the National DNA Database, but it would take a few weeks. "That's fine, thanks for letting me know," she said as she hung up the call, pulled her burger out of the bag and took a large hungry bite out of it, and headed back in the direction of the station.

Coming back into the station, she handed over a burger and some fries out of the bag to Bates, and handed him over a can of pop. "Cheers, Gov," he said and started tucking in. McColl went back into her office and sat back down. Flicking through the papers on her desk, she sipped her own can of pop when Bates brought his lunch into her office. "Mind if I join you?"

She looked up and smiled. "Course not, come in." She moved some things out of the way on one side of the desk for Bates to put his lunch down. He pulled a chair over and sat down.

"What you reading up on?" he asked with interest.

"Pull the door over, would you?" she replied, taking another swig of her drink. After Bates did as she had asked she said, "Do you remember that shooting case on Rosendale Avenue?"

Bates thought for a moment, then responded, "Do you mean the double shooting that was never solved?" She nodded.

"Well, I think I may have found a way of linking Ryan Reynolds to the crime scene."

Bates' eyes widened with excitement. McColl explained about the altercation at Matthew's birthday party and her silk scarf. Bates suddenly looked troubled and frowned. "But don't we need someone's consent to run checks on their DNA?" Sounding worried, he continued. "What if we do even establish a match? How do we go about bringing him in?"

McColl smiled cunningly. "We find a way to get Ryan to provide a DNA swab with his saliva." Bates still wasn't convinced.

"How though? We can't just rock up and take swabs!"

McColl smiled, and said, "We can if we're requesting all males within a certain age bracket provide a swab for process of elimination from our investigation."

Bates smiled and nodded, but then added, "But what if he doesn't consent and refuses to take a swab?"

McColl smiled and said, "Then we find another way." She sipped at her drink then added, "Besides, he might not even throw up a match, but it's worth a try. Narcotics can't pin anything on him, he's definitely thick as thieves with that Ken Allington though, I've done some homework on him. Ken's been like a father figure to him whilst he was growing up. I think they're probably serving up drugs together, but we just need to prove it." Before Bates could ask another question, reading his thoughts she continued, "And if our friend Ken does know anything about either Molly's murder or Heidi's disappearance then at least we'll establish either a motive or a lead."

Chapter 23

It was a dark Wednesday evening in February 1998, and John was at home in the living room watching TV. He was flicking through some papers for work when Kirsty came downstairs and joined him.

"Hi Dad," Kirsty said cheerfully. "How was your day?" John looked up from what he was doing and smiled at his daughter.

"Yeah, it was good thanks, we secured a new contract today," John said happily.

Kirsty smiled. "Oh, that's good, is your job OK now?"

He smiled and said, "Well things are looking up, put it that way."

Kirsty went and sat on the other sofa and picked up a TV magazine; flicking through it but not really reading it she said without looking up, "So will you be celebrating with your lady friend the copper?" She laughed teasingly. John laughed as well.

"Oh it's not like that, we're just good friends." He smiled. "She's a good listener."

Kirsty put the magazine down and looked over at her dad. Changing her approach, she said gently, "Listen Dad, it is OK if you're seeing someone, if she makes you happy that's all that matters. I say go for it."

John blushed a bit and smiled, but repeated himself. "We're just good friends. I'm seeing her on Saturday to help her put some shelves up."

Kirsty laughed despite herself. "Oh really? Can't she put them up by herself?"

John laughed and replied in a sing-song voice, "No, she can't, a shelf needs two pairs of hands." Kirsty laughed along. "What about you?" John asked, changing the subject. "You up to much over the weekend?"

Kirsty smiled and said vaguely, "Yeah, maybe. Marlon said we could go for a drive."

John sat up and replied, "Oh really?" genuinely

interested but also slightly concerned. "Where are you driving to?"

Kirsty picked the TV magazine back up and began flicking through it again. Picking up the TV remote control she started flicking through the channels. After a couple of minutes Kirsty replied, "Oh, just to a small town in Edenbridge. Now the weather's brightening up a bit we thought we'd get some fresh farm produce and go for a picnic."

John listened and hesitated before replying again, "Kirsty, I thought you said you were done with him?"

She looked over at her dad and innocently said, "Oh, I meant it, we're just good friends."

*

DCI Sally McColl was at home dressed in her favourite weekend outfit, soft jeans with a red and white checked shirt. She was sitting on the stairs putting on her black ankle boots when the doorbell went. She pulled the zips up the inside of each boot and went to answer the front door, checking the spy hole before opening the door; it was John. She smiled as she opened the door. "Hi John, you're right on time."

John smiled and gave her a box of cream cakes. "Something to keep us going when we're putting the shelves up." McColl smiled and took the cakes from him.

"Thank you, what a great idea, I'll stick them in the fridge." She walked through to the kitchen and John followed behind her, looking around with interest at what a police officer's house looked like. The house was crisp and clean looking. John looked briefly into the magnolia living room as he walked past the door; apart from a few books on the bookshelf in the living room, the house was minimalistic. The hallway was a light green colour with an emerald green and brown border in the middle of it. The kitchen was a pale yellow colour with grey granite surfaces. The kitchen looked fairly new and had an appearance of hardly ever being used.

"It's a nice place you've got here," John said appreciatively. McColl smiled as she closed the fridge door.

"Thanks, I've been doing bits and pieces to the place, but it still needs a lot of work." She pointed at the shelves which were on the table to one side of the kitchen.

John went over and picked up the pack of screws; he shook his head and remarked, "It looks like you're missing a bracket, and you're going to need some bigger screws than this, otherwise the whole thing will collapse after a couple of months."

She sighed. "Oh, really? These are the parts that came with the shelf."

John smiled. "Yeah, they always put the smaller ones in, but they don't hold much weight." He put the packet down. "There's a hardware store on the high street, we could pop down there before we start?"

McColl smiled and sighed. "OK, I'll grab my coat."

They left McColl's house and got into John's red Volkswagen Scirocco. "Nice car," McColl laughed. He grinned as he put his seatbelt on.

"I've had it years, it's reliable and big enough for being out and about with the kids." She smiled as she put her seatbelt on. John started up the engine and noticed the fuel tank was running low. "Oh, looks like I'm going to have to fill her up, there's a garage opposite the hardware store." John checked his mirrors, signalled and moved the car out onto the road.

As they were driving along McColl thought out loud, "I'll head over to the shop and meet you in there."

"OK," John replied, concentrating on the road.

As they pulled into the garage, John pulled up by

one of the pumps and put the handbrake on. He switched off the engine and went around to the pump. "I'll see you over there," McColl said as she headed out towards the high street. She approached the crossing and looked both ways; as she was crossing she noticed a beige car pulling into the garage and pull up behind John's car. She was just about to walk into the shop but out of the corner of her eye she noticed John's reaction to the car; something was bothering him but McColl couldn't see who it was that was in the car. It looked like the same type of car that had been involved in the Rosendale Avenue shootings, but she couldn't be sure. McColl waited a minute or so and took her mobile phone out. As she looked back up she recognised the familiar face of the young lad who was exiting the vehicle, it was Ryan Reynolds. Tapping her phone against her lips, she watched with interest. Dialling Bates' number she waited patiently for her call to be answered, but it went through to voicemail. "Bates, it's me, McColl. When you get this can you do me a favour? I need to know the make of the car that was involved in the Rosendale Avenue shootings, was it an Austin Allegro, if so can you confirm the make and colour. Also, is there any news on the DNA lab results, call me when you get this; If I don't answer, leave me a voicemail and I'll call when I can talk."

She put her Motorola away and went into the hardware store. Her mind was running overtime. What had she just seen in John's reaction? His body language had completely changed when he had seen that car. Picking up some packets of screws she absentmindedly started comparing them. "I can see this isn't a social call," Frank said as he looked over the counter. "I hardly recognised you in your jeans," he smiled. McColl forced a smile back.

"No, just doing some DIY," she said in a sing-song response.

"Do you need any help or do you know what you're looking for over there?" Frank asked helpfully.

"Oh I think I'm OK thanks, my friend will be here in a minute, he knows what to get."

Just then the bell went as the door to the shop opened. John came over and started looking at the brackets. "Think these are the brackets you need, and these are probably the best screws to attach them."

Casually McColl replied, "OK, thanks. What are your kids up to today? John looked up at her briefly, wondering where this was heading.

"Oliver will probably be in his room, and Kirsty's

meeting up with a friend, they're going on a picnic."

Approaching the counter to pay, McColl replied with interest, "Should be a nice day for a picnic, where's she going to?"

Frank rang up the items on the till, as John got his wallet out of his back pocket. "Erm, I think she said she's going to Edenbridge."

Frank stopped and listened carefully without looking up. "Edenbridge?" McColl exclaimed. "That's a bit of a way to go," she remarked.

John smiled and shook his head, and continued, "Yeah Kirsty's meeting a friend, and they're taking a drive out there together. Now she's passed her driving test maybe she's enjoying her freedom." He smiled as he counted some money and handed it across to Frank. "I think that should be right, but you can check it if you like."

Frank, who was standing still, looked at John and replied, "Which friend?"

John, who wasn't expecting the question, was confused. "Huh? What do you mean?" he replied.

"Which friend?" Frank repeated. "Was it Marlon…?"

John was surprised. "Well actually, yes I think it

was, but what's it to you?" he responded, slightly annoyed.

Frank swallowed hard, before slowly replying, "Marlon's my nephew. I think your daughter and my nephew are checking up on Ken Allington. He's been asking a lot of questions about Ken's land out there." McColl raised her eyebrows and breathed out heavily.

"Well if they are, they would be trespassing. I'm not sure if Ken will be too happy about them snooping about on his private land."

Frank nodded. "He does have quite a temper on him."

John shook his head and took his mobile out of his pocket, saying, "Kirsty's a sensible girl, I'll call her, tell her not to go onto his land." After a couple of minutes of ringing, the phone went through to voicemail; frustrated, he put his phone back in his pocket. "Do you have a number for Marlon?"

Frank went to the landline on the wall he frowned as he dialled Marlon's number; after a couple of minutes he put the receiver back on the wall. "It's no use, he's not picking up." Frank said, sounding worried. They stood in silence for what seemed like an eternity.

McColl then said, "John, you remember when

Kirsty came to see me a while ago, she was convinced Ken had something to do with what happened to Molly. Do you think she still does?"

John frowned, then sighed. "Well even if she's wrong Ken's not going to be happy about the two of them prying and snooping on his land." Then his face darkened, as he added, "And if she's right then they could both be in danger. Frank, where's Ken's land?"

Chapter 24

Marlon and Kirsty were driving down a country road in Edenbridge. Marlon was driving. "I think this is it just down there on the right," Kirsty said, as Marlon slowed the car down and turned right down a narrow country lane. The trees were getting thicker the further down they drove. They had taken food and supplies with them, and had already stopped a while back and had eaten most of the sandwiches. On the backseat they had torches, a blanket and a few other emergency supplies. Marlon looked out of the window as the weather became overcast. *The late afternoon sun won't last long*, he thought to himself. Beginning to regret the trip he sighed, "OK, what do we do now?" as the car could go no further. "We take a look around, see if anyone's about," Kirsty replied.

"If the coast is clear we get closer to the old barn house if it's still there." It was gone 3pm in the afternoon of early February and the sun disappeared behind the clouds.

"Listen, are you sure about this?" Marlon asked hesitantly, thinking about his university course he had just started. "I mean we're trespassing on private property. I don't want to risk getting thrown of my course it'll ruin my career prospects if we get arrested - yours too!"

Kirsty shrugged, irritated. "Marlon, it's fine," she replied. "There's probably nobody about and nobody will see us or know we were ever here," she said calmly. Kirsty gingerly removed her seatbelt and slowly climbed out of the car. Reluctantly, Marlon followed her. They had parked in the entrance to a field just inside of a lay-by off the main road. They had driven the car as far as they could go; they were met with some bushes and a stile. Kirsty put one foot up on the stile and climbed over. Marlon climbed over after her. The distant sound of cars gradually disappeared as they walked further into the woodlands.

"Kirsty are you sure we're in the right place?" Marlon pressed on. "This might not even be Ken's land."

Kirsty turned and smiled. "It isn't," she laughed, and then carried on walking, and pointed ahead of her, "but it is his land over there." She walked further into the woods until they came to another stile. She climbed over, with Marlon behind her. Marlon was confused; during the drive he had thought all these places looked the same to him, all fields surrounded by either trees, heather fields or woodland. Some fields had a few sheep; then further along some had some cows, but most of the fields appeared to be stretched out for miles, without any signs of life. As they walked into another field Kirsty said quietly; "When we were growing up, Mum used to talk about this area and the places they played in as kids. I remember Mum showed us some old photos years ago, then after she died, we would often go through them over the years; there's a stream by an old farmhouse somewhere around here. That's the part of the land I thought Mum had said Ken that had sold, and that's how he could afford to buy the bar; I'll bet that's the part he's kept hold of."

Sure enough, the sound of the grass and branches cracking underneath their feet, Marlon began to hear running water, which sounded like it was coming from a stream. As they walked further along, in the distance they saw what appeared to be an old barn; it appeared to be derelict and had an old tractor parked inside it, with a couple of old tyres leaning up against it. It appeared to have been there for some time, as there was woodland growing around the tyres. The place was giving Marlon the creeps, and already thinking this was a bad idea, he grabbed Kirsty's arm. "Come on, let's go, it's starting to get dark. Why don't we come back another time while it's still light?"

Kirsty stopped and looked up at him. "Look Marlon, go back and wait by the car if you're scared. I'm going to case the joint, I'm not ready to leave just yet." Taking out the torch from her jacket pocket, she switched it on and stomped off in the direction of the old barn. Marlon sighed and chased after her.

"Kirsty! Kirsty wait for me!" he hissed after her.

They walked past an old, brown, wooden sign which was rotting away. The sign had some faded writing on which read 'Old Codgers Yard'. Kirsty looked up at it and said, "Yes, this is definitely the place." They walked into the old barn; there was nothing there apart from some broken furniture, and an old wooden chair which was tipped on its side with one leg missing. Kirsty noticed an old pair of boots by the side of the barn; they looked old and hard-worn.

Marlon noticed a switch on the wall; he went over

and clicked it a couple of times, but to no avail, no lights came on. "Oh well," he said, thinking to himself there was no sign that anybody had been there in years. Smiling with satisfaction, Marlon laughed. "You see? There's nothing here. Come on let's get out of here." He went to pull Kirsty's arm to go, but Kirsty gasped, "Did you hear that?"

Marlon froze. "Hear what?" he asked, his voice alive with fear.

"I thought I heard something." They both stayed still and listened; the shuffling noise had stopped. Marlon looked down at the floor. "It sounded like it was underneath us," he remarked.

Kirsty shrugged him off and walked towards something. She turned on her torch and shone it down on the floor where something glistened under the light. Slowly, she walked across to the silver object which had caught her attention. *What was that?* she wondered. Kicking away the reeds which were surrounding it, Kirsty realised it was a silver ring, which was attached to what appeared to be a trap door. She pulled but the door would not budge. She traced her fingers around the door. "Marlon, there's something down there," Kirsty said with bated breath. Her fingers stumbled across a lock, which was secured by a padlock. "Marlon, can you grab a brick or something?"

"A brick?" He sounded incredulous.

"Yeah, or something heavy," she replied.

Marlon looked around him, and found an old metal rod. "Well I can't find a brick but this should do the trick!" he said, feeling proud of himself. Getting to work, Marlon knelt down and pushed the end of the rod through the loop in the padlock, he pulled the rod from one side then to the other, the padlock which was old and rusty, creaked noisily as Marlon forced the lock open. Getting up, Marlon leaned on the wall; as he did so his hands felt something sharp. "Shit!" he said, pulling his hand away. Whatever it was had cut the skin and he winced as he felt the warm flow of blood oozing out of his hand.

Kirsty pulled some tissue out of her pocket. "Here," she said. "Use this for now."

"Thanks," Marlon replied. "What do you think is down there?"

Kirsty looked up at Marlon, and said seriously, "I don't know but there's only one way to find out." As he looked at Kirsty, Marlon felt a surge of emotion for her. Considering they hadn't known each other for very long he knew he was falling for her; her courage amazed him, she was fearless. Not in a million years would he be here while it was getting dark on a whim that they might find something, with a girl he hardly knew.

"What?" Kirsty asked, looking up at him, puzzled.

"Nothing, let's see what's down there then."

As they pulled the door open, they strained their eyes to see what was down there. As their eyes adjusted to the darkness, there appeared to be a dark staircase. Kirsty started to walk down the staircase; as she was halfway down she stopped and could not believe the sight before her. Lying at the bottom of the stairs with her hands and legs chained was what appeared to be a young woman. "Heidi Perthwaite!" Kirsty gasped. Sure enough, the girl was in bad shape, but Heidi was alive.

Marlon, who had started to follow Kirsty down the old wooden staircase, was unaware of a figure approaching him from behind; wielding the rusty metal rod Marlon had used to force the padlock to the trapdoor open. It was raised above his head and its impact sent Marlon flying down the stairs, narrowly missing Kirsty who had instinctively stood to one side. She turned to see who was there; the dark shadow was towering above her at the entrance to the trap door, and she charged back up the stairs and pushed past the person and ran as fast as she could around the barn house. The man who had not been prepared for her reaction, had slammed the trap door shut, and dragged a bag of fertilizer over to wedge it shut. *How did he know we were there?* Kirsty thought to herself as she charged back through the woods. Turning over her shoulder she saw the silhouette of someone in hot pursuit chasing after her.

*

Inside the cellar, Marlon had started to come around. His vision was blurry but in his hazy state he could make out a shape in the darkness, of a frightened young woman, who was dirty, and thin like she had not had a decent meal in a long time. As she turned her head up towards the light, he blue eyes twinkled with fear in the darkness. Her hair was long, and hung in a messy heap around her shoulders. She was wearing a blanket around her and what appeared to be a long white dress which was tattered and dirty.

"I guess you must be Heidi, I'm Marlon," he slurred in the darkness awkwardly.

The girl's hesitant response was raspy and dry. "Y-Yes. Why are you here? Have you come to save me?" Her voice was a whisper. Marlon tried to pull himself up to sitting, but he was too dizzy, so he slumped back down onto his side.

He coughed, as he answered, "You could say that."

Heidi looked at Marlon and replied, "You need to be careful, there have been others, and Ken saw to it and got rid of them."

Marlon was stunned. *Who else has been down here?* he thought to himself. His mind was reeling. "How?" he responded.

Heidi dragged herself onto her side and pulled herself up to sitting. She helped Marlon up against the wall. "There were two of them to begin with…" She began to speak and her voice broke into tears. "The other one was a police officer," she said through her tears. Marlon gasped with horror. Heidi continued, "But they had an argument one day and after that I never saw the other one again. Ken said he'd rigged his car, and there'd been an accident, so I wouldn't be seeing him again." Marlon couldn't believe what he was hearing. Heidi sighed and took a deep breath. Her voice was stronger as she swallowed and took control of her emotions as she continued. "Then, somebody else found out I was down here. So Ken caught them before they could tell anyone; he tied them up down here with me for a couple of weeks, till he was no use to him and then he shot him. He's buried in one of the fields, or so Ken told me. He said if I ever tried to escape I'd be joining him."

Marlon didn't know what to say, but in a voice full of conviction he replied, "Now listen here, we're going to get you out of here. We're both going to get out of here alive. My girlfriend's out there now and she'll be getting us help." Heidi seemed so cold and emotionless as she replied with a voice that had let hope go a long time ago. "Your girlfriend is probably already dead."

*

Kirsty made it back to the car and climbed in. As she started the engine and reversed back in a circle to face the other way, a figure stood stock still in front of the car, with gripped fists. Ken took two steps towards here and shouted out, "It wasn't me! But I know who did kill Molly." Kirsty gasped as her hands gripped the steering wheel. Her mind was racing as she hesitated. Ken continued to take another step towards the car as he shouted out, "And if you kill me, you'll never find out who murdered your precious sister!" He laughed wickedly as he took another step towards the car.

Kirsty's eyes blazed with rage. "LIAR!" she growled and put her foot on the accelerator. The car sped towards Ken and caught his left side as he went to dive out of the way. She stopped the car and turned to look in the direction he had gone in the darkness. She thought of Marlon and Heidi. She couldn't just leave them there. *I need to get help,* she thought. *I have to get help.* She flipped open the glove compartment and took out the large kitchen knife which she had stashed there, wrapped in a tea-towel. Putting it on her lap, she went to drive the car in the direction of the road. Kirsty screamed as she heard the sound of gunshots hitting the car. Instinctively she covered her head with her hands, while the car was still moving. The petrol tank took a hit; instinctively she grabbed the knife and dived out of the moving vehicle into dusk which was setting in as the car she had been travelling in exploded into flames behind her. Kirsty rolled a few times before landing down in a ditch a few meters away.

Chapter 25

John's car was about three miles away from Ken's barn. It was getting dark and he was starting to worry. "What was she thinking driving all the way out here?" John muttered to himself.

Just then, McColl's mobile went. "It's probably work," she said, hitting the switch so the call went straight through to voicemail. "If it's important they'll leave a message." She smiled. John looked at his fuel tank.

"I'll need to get some more fuel, I didn't fill up the tank because I didn't know we'd be driving so far."

McColl frowned. "OK, well, probably better to get some as soon as we see a garage, we don't know when the next one will be." John nodded. After another mile or so they saw the bright lights of a garage.

"I'll fill up the tank this time," John laughed. As he went and filled up, McColl took the opportunity to use the ladies'. When she came out of the cubicle, she took her mobile out of her pocket and listened to the voicemail message; it was from Bates.

"Hi Gov, yes the model of the car from Rosendale Avenue was a beige Austin Allegro, and as for the DNA match, well, it was for one of the live cases, but not the one you would think. The DNA sample was a match for the case of Molly Symmonds."

McColls eyes widened as she exited the toilets she stopped walking, mentally piecing things together in her mind. At that moment, John came out of the garage. "Is everything alright?" he called over looking concerned. Deleting the voicemail, she joined John at the car.

McColl forced a smile. "Yeah, I'm just tired," she replied. "Let's go get your daughter and call it a night, think the shelves will have to wait till another time." John nodded in agreement and they drove in silence towards Ken's land.

John thought back to the days when he and his wife Lisa had been dating. They had driven out this way a couple of times over the years, before the kids came along. Lisa had said it reminded her of her youth. His wife had told John about games of hide and seek she had played as a youngster with her friends; back then there was hardly anything there, apart from the old barn house which was in use to tend to the land. John decided to drive over there as there really wasn't much else around that way. As the car took the turning on the right off the main road, John pulled up by the stile. As they got out of the car McColl coughed. "I can smell smoke."

John sniffed the air and agreed. "Where's it coming from?"

McColl walked over to the stile and climbed up on it. "I think it's over that way," she said, pointing towards the woodland as she climbed over the fence. "Quick, let's go!"

John scrambled over the stile behind her as they darted through the woods in the direction of the barn house.

Chapter 26

Kirsty was grazed and bruised from the fall but was otherwise OK; she clambered up to her feet, looking around herself frantically; she strained to see or hear where Ken was. Unable to see him or hear where Ken was, she listened again. The afternoon sun had disappeared; where it was overcast it was beginning to get dark. Hearing only the rustling and crackling of her burning car, Kirsty crept back towards the barn house. She approached the trap door and heaved the heavy bag of fertiliser out of the way. Kirsty swung the trap door open. She crept back down the stairs. "Marlon!" she whispered desperately into the darkness. "Marlon!"

"Over here!"

Recognising Marlon's voice, Kirsty heaved a sigh of relief and ran in the direction of where Marlon and Heidi were on the floor of the basement.

"See, I told you she would come back!" Marlon said, directed at Heidi.

Kirsty hugged him to her, asking, "How badly are you hurt? We need to get out of here now, Marlon, Ken's got a gun! He's just shot at me in the car and it's exploded!"

Marlon's eyes widened in the darkness in disbelief. "Is that what that noise was?!" Kirsty nodded in response.

"I don't know how, but we've got to get access to another vehicle," she exclaimed frantically. As Heidi moved the shackles she was attached to jangled in the darkness. "Heidi, where does Ken keep the keys?"

Heidi looked up at her in the darkness, and said sadly, "In his pocket, they're always attached to his trousers."

Thinking desperately, Kirsty asked, "How far does the chain go?" Heidi stood up shakily.

"I can move about down here but that's as far as I can get to." She walked over to where a tin bath stood, which had a bucket beside it.

Kirsty gasped. *How long has the poor woman been down here?* she thought to herself. Taking stock, she swallowed nervously, and said with determination, "OK, right, well you won't be spending another night down here, we're going to get you out of here."

They hushed as they heard the slopping of liquid above them; it dripped through the floorboards to below where they were huddled together. The strong smell of petrol pervaded their senses. Marlon staggered to his feet. "We've got to get those keys – now!" Marlon darted towards the stairs, and staggered up them, holding onto the wall as he clambered up in the darkness, just as Ken appeared, towering over him at the top of the stairs. Mustering all his strength, Marlon took a deep breath and growled as he dived towards Ken's waist, grabbing him as he did so. Ken fell backwards, losing his balance. The gun went off as both men fell to the ground.

"Marlon!" Kirsty screamed and charged back up the stairs. As she came out of the basement, she surveyed the scene before her. In the dusk light she could just make out Ken was lying still, pinned to the floor. Marlon was lying on top of him and there was a pool of blood around them. Marlon's hand rustled against a groaning Ken; locating the keys, he detached the key ring and threw the bunch towards Kirsty.

"Here, catch!" he sighed.

Kirsty grabbed the bunch of keys and made her way frantically back down to where Heidi was chained up. Her hands were shaking as she fumbled the keys against the lock; the first couple wouldn't fit. "Come on! Please!" Heidi pleaded, with gritted teeth, her voice breaking with anticipation and fear. The third key fit and as the lock was released, she shrieked with hysteria. Kirsty tried the same key on the second lock, but it didn't work.

Frustrated, Kirsty felt for a key of a similar size in the darkness. "Bingo!" she exclaimed as she put the key in the second lock; it released with a noisy clank. Heidi was crying with emotion as Kirsty took her hand and led her up the stairs. They went over to where Marlon was, but he couldn't stand up. Suddenly realising he was badly injured, Kirsty took Marlon's left arm and put it around her neck, and Heidi took the other arm and did the same on the other side. They made their way out of the barn steadily. As they came outside and headed towards the trees, neither of them noticed Ken was also now on his feet, coming up behind them.

*

"That's Kirsty's car!" John shouted as they passed the

vehicle which was still in flames.

McColl ran towards it. Shielding her face from the flames with her arm, she said, "I can't see if there was anyone in it!" Hearing a gunshot come from the direction of the barn, they ran towards it, noticing three figures coming towards them through the trees. McColl also noticed another figure hobbling after the trio. She pulled her jacket back and pulled out her own handgun. Flicking the safety lock off; she aimed her gun over the group's shoulders and stared down the barrel. Recognising his daughter, John shouted, "Kirsty!" and rushed towards them.

"There's someone behind them!" McColl shouted.

"Dad! Dad! Help us, please help us, he's crazy, Ken's crazy!" Kirsty shouted as John ran towards them.

"Ken, I've got a gun and it's loaded, so stop right there, it's over."

Ignoring McColl, Ken hobbled towards them with his own gun still in his hand. "You fucking bitch!" he shouted, spittle hanging from his mouth. Ken aimed and shot in the direction of the three figures he was chasing. Marlon collapsed to the ground. As he went down, Heidi ran towards McColl. McColl could not believe the sight before her. *Is this Heidi Perthwaite?* she wondered incredulously.

As Heidi made it over to McColl, McColl pulled the frail young woman protectively behind her as she aimed the gun. She fired at Ken, twice. He dropped to the ground and lay motionless a few metres away.

"Marlon! Oh no, he's badly hurt!" Kirsty said. "Quick, phone an ambulance!" She cradled Marlon's head in her lap. "Just hold on, Marlon, we're going to get you help," she whispered through tears kindly as she stroked his hair in her lap.

"Kirsty, Kirsty," Marlon whispered to her. "I need to tell you something. It was Ryan."

Confused, Kirsty carried on stroking his hair. "What was Ryan?" she asked.

"…Molly," was the last thing Marlon said before he lost consciousness.

John, who had heard this, raged, "I knew that boy had something to do with it! Why didn't he tell us this before?!"

McColl, who was dialling the number for the emergency services, listened with interest. Kirsty was stunned as she sat there in silence, with Marlon's head still resting in her lap. The police arrived and John stood in the darkness in silent rage, as the paramedics tended to Marlon, and Heidi. They had put a blanket around Kirsty's shoulders and she waited in a daze outside the back of the ambulance.

McColl came up behind John. Without waiting for him to look around, she said, "You knew it was Ryan who killed Molly, didn't you John?" John stood there in silence and didn't respond. "Is that why you shot that couple on Rosendale Avenue, because you thought it was his car?" John turned around slowly in shock; his face was of confusion and surprise. "It was you, wasn't it John?"

Turning to face McColl but not looking up, he asked, "How did you know?"

She replied, "Oh I didn't know, not for sure." She paused, then continued, "I guess you could say there were signs."

John sighed, and slumped down to the floor. He was so tired and weary. The lines on his face, his aging complexion and greying hair all told their own story, of the toll of years living with grief. John heaved another sigh, relaxed his shoulders and gave up. Taking the opportunity whilst his guard was down, McColl asked him; "Where is it, John? What did you do with the gun?"

He sighed. *What would be the point of withholding information at this stage?* he mused to himself. "It's in the Canal by Mercury Way." There was a silent moment between them, before he went on. "It's a relief to finally not have to hide it anymore," John admitted. "I've got to live with what I've done and I'm not sure I know how," he said sadly.

"John, you're grieving, the courts will see that. I'm not saying that what you've done is OK or right, but even if it had of been Ryan's car that night, even if you had of shot him instead, you would still have to live with what you've done."

John shrugged, and said, "Yeah, but at least it would have been worth it." The sirens in the distance started to grow louder. John looked up at DCI McColl and said, "I'll come clean, tell the truth, it's time." They sat in silence and waited for the cavalry to arrive.

Chapter 27

Molly's murder trial went to court in autumn 1999. Ryan had been remanded in custody without bail, much to the protest of his parents. They would not believe their son would be responsible for Molly's murder. So even with all the DNA evidence, in his ignorance, Ryan pleaded not guilty, which when he was eventually found guilty, unanimously by a jury of twelve, went against him. The prosecution argued that Ryan was cold, calculating and had traits of psychopathic tendencies. Growing up, Ryan had never seeing much of his father, as he worked away a lot on business. Ryan's mother had expensive taste and had never provided much in the way of love and affection. As a result of this, Ryan had been passed around to various paid nannies growing up; this had led to him being lonely, isolated, and emotionally stunted.

Ken had stepped into the father figure role which Ryan's parents knew nothing about, until the trial. Ken did not survive the shootings at the barn. Prior to his demise, Ken had also had control issues around women, following years of living with an abusive father during his own childhood, Ken had craved adulation, which nothing could satisfy, a need which could not be ignored when he came across Heidi Perthwaite.

Ryan had become influenced by Ken and although he was not aware of Heidi being in captivity, and despite his parents paying a good lawyer to represent him in court, he still received a life sentence for Molly's murder. Plus an additional eight-year sentence for dealing in cocaine, for Ken, which also came out during the trial. Even after the trial, Ryan's parents continued to dispute the rulings, and argued that it was all a miscarriage of justice, concentrating all their time, money and energy in building an appeal case. A case which took years to return to court.

*

The details of Heidi Perthwaite's kidnapping unfolded in the months that followed. Where Ken had not survived, Heidi pieced together what she could recall from her fractured memories of a Sunday evening over summer where her life was changed forever. Ken had seen Heidi leaving the park in tears. He had been selling some cocaine wraps to a local business man. As opportunity would have it, they had been and left early. Ken was about to drive off when he must have seen Heidi coming through the park at a distance. Taking pity on the poor distressed girl, he convinced her to have a joint with him in his car. Heidi had seen Ken with Joe so she recognised him. Ken had said she needed to 'calm herself down, her parents wouldn't want to see her in such a state'. After having a smoke with Ken, Heidi had decided to go back to the park to confront Kieran about being unfaithful. However by the time Heidi came back to the park where the climbing frame was, the gang had dispersed and the park was empty. Thinking his luck was in, Ken at first tried to seduce the emotional and vulnerable teenage girl, but when that didn't work, a scuffle ensued. Ken hit the girl over the head with the back end of an empty bottle of cider. That was the last thing Heidi remembered, before waking up in the boot of Ken's car. Ken later told Heidi he had burned down the climbing frame to get rid of any evidence. Heidi was taken straight to the barn and had not been seen since.

Joe Allington and his mum Carly came forwards

during the aftermath when everything hit the national newspapers. Joe had been terrified of Ken and knew his uncle was friends with Harold Spencer. Fearful for both himself and his mum, Carly had the opportunity of moving to America. Joe couldn't wait to convince his mum that they should take it and go. However, the memory of Heidi had haunted him and had cast a shadow over the years that followed. One day his mum had found Joe crying watching the news. It was only then that Joe confided in her. Carly convinced Joe they should contact the police and speak up. They flew back to the UK and cooperated with the police's investigation.

*

The double shooting on Rosendale Avenue went to trial in the winter of 1999, just before the Millennium. John spent the time of celebrations remanded in custody. He pleaded guilty to both shootings. John was also found guilty by a jury of twelve. He also received a life sentence for double murder; the prosecution stated the case was aggravated because of the use of a firearm as well as the shootings being premeditated. The jury decided it was on the grounds of diminished responsibility, and as one of the victims of the shooting was linked to a drugs ring, which the police managed to bring down as a result of the shootings, he was also sentenced to life in prison. The trial judge recommended a minimum of twenty years should be served before he could be considered for parole. John kept Oliver's name out of the investigation and remained consistent in his account that neither of his sons knew about what he had done. Only Oliver and John ever really knew the full story behind the shootings.

The court heard that John had been a family man, who had a good job, with no previous offences. Then his life had started to fall apart following the loss of his wife to cancer. Losing his mother-in-law and just over a year later losing his daughter in such a brutal way, had tipped him over the edge. The defence argued that John had a long-standing undiagnosed mental health disorder for which he was willing to seek the appropriate help.

John's case was helped by the result being that a young woman was rescued from captivity, and reunited with her long-suffering mother, who had never given up hope of finding her daughter alive and made a point of being vocal with the national press that if it wasn't for John and McColl following Kirsty and Marlon to the barn, not only would she never have found her daughter but it would have been unlikely the three of them would have made it out alive if Ken had had his way. Marlon also testified in court that John was probably the only reason he and the others had made it out of the barn alive, which helped his case.

Chapter 28

2010, HMP London, England

John lifted his head up from his pillow, as the cell door was banged three times. "Visitors for you," came the booming voice through the door, interrupting his thoughts. He sat up and rubbed his face.

"Thanks. OK, I'm coming."

John followed the prison warden through the corridors and round to the visitors' hall. The vast space opened up to a large enclosed area that had various tables and chairs scattered about. There was a mix of groups of families, couples, some with children. Many of the faces were happy and there was an air of rare positive energy and cheerful voices. John scanned the hall, until he settled on a table over on the far side, where he saw some familiar faces.

"Dad!" Oliver called out, as he went over.

John went to hug his son, before being rudely interrupted by one of the wardens who came in between them. "No physical contact. Come on, John, you know the rules."

John looked up at Dave; he was one of the nicer wardens. "Sure, sure, sorry, just excited to see my kids."

Dave smiled sympathetically but shook his head. "Just take your seats, please."

John nodded and sat down. He looked across the table at Oliver, Kirsty and Matthew. "So, how are you holding up, Dad?" Matthew asked with concern in his eyes.

John chuckled good-naturedly. "Oh, you know me, must'n' grumble." He shrugged. "How about you all, what you all been up to?"

Matthew, Oliver and Kirsty looked up at each other briefly, then back at their Dad. Oliver answered for all of them; "We're good Dad, just want to make sure you're OK," he smiled affectionately.

John chuckled. "Worried about me? Why? I'm fine. Nearly finished my art course." He smiled at his children across the table. They were all so grown up now. Over the years they had made sure they held on to the family home. Each had made an effort to pay their dad regular visits, and on the odd occasion, like today, they all came together, and it made John's heart sing with joy when they did so. Over the years, John had tried his hands at various classes to pass the time, from pottery, to a couple of GCSE classes, and an A-Level was also now under his belt. The art class was his favourite though; he enjoyed an outlet for his emotions and giving his artwork to his family when they visited him. John's latest piece was a painting of his family all together, and he had been working on it for months as a Christmas present for them. John had also been working on another painting, this one was of DCI Sally McColl; he had passed it onto the wardens, to give to his children to arrange to get the piece to her. John had not seen McColl since the trial, though he had thought of her often over the years. He had always hoped that one day, she would come and visit him, but she had stayed away. John had heard that Sally McColl had done rather well as a result of the investigation, and her career had soared. He was happy for her, but missed talking to her. During their brief time together, John had become fond of her, and under different circumstances, he felt in his heart, they may have had a future together. This was not going to happen now, and with a heavy heart, he had accepted this. John had also heard that she had been instrumental in helping Heidi to rebuild her life, and for this he was incredibly proud of her.

Chapter 29

2019, London, England

John was in front of the parole board. The result had gone in his favour. In a few weeks' time, although he would be on tag for the first year, John was on his way to becoming a free man.

The weeks flew by. As John collected his brown bag from the guard at the reception, the warden tipped his hat at John. "Goodbye John, and good luck." John sighed, and smiled as he walked through the large heavy doors into the brilliant white sunshine. As he heard the doors slam shut behind him, he looked around. He was a free man.

Unsure of how he felt at being outside after twenty years, he walked slowly towards the end of the dirt track. He noticed a car was waiting for him, with the engine running. The passenger door opened, and his daughter Kirsty stepped out. She smiled at him and walked slowly towards him. Squeezing her dad into a big hug she said, "Time to come home, Dad."

Realising there was somebody else in the car, he looked over his daughter's shoulder. Turning, they both looked over at the car. The driver's door opened on the other side of the car, and a head popped up. Leaning on the roof of the car, a voice said, "Hello stranger. So are you getting in or did you want to walk home?" John's face was a picture of confusion, which turned to realisation when he realised he recognised the voice.

"DCI McColl, what are you doing here?"

Kirsty laughed. "She's here to take you home, Dad."

McColl smiled. "Thank you for my painting." John blushed.

"I wasn't sure you had received it," he admitted.

McColl continued smiling and said, "I did, and I loved it." John nodded and smiled back.

Looking at his daughter, he said, "Since when did you two become friends anyway?"

Kirsty opened the passenger door for her dad and

then opened the back door of the car and got in, replying vaguely, "Oh, a while now. Oh, and Dad, McColl's no longer with the force now."

John walked over to the car. McColl smiled, and nodded her head. "I had a better offer." Then she looked down at the car and said, "But your daughter is now."

John was confused. "What do you mean?" he asked, trying to catch up. McColl laughed.

"Let's get you home, there's lots to catch up on."

END

ABOUT THE AUTHOR

I am Tracy Ryden, my maiden name was Strain. I am thirty-nine years old, have been married to my husband Joel for eleven years and a mother of two boys; Archie who is nine and Chris who is four.

I have worked for the NHS for eighteen years and I am currently employed full-time as a HR Advisor in one of the world's leading teaching hospitals in London.

I do a lot of writing in my day-to-day job, and growing up I always enjoyed creative writing. Occasionally I would write short stories, particularly ghost stories, and also some poetry. On a few occasions I wrote rhymes for our Parish newsletter, *The Borough Piper*, and for a short spell I was in the Borough Bagpipe Band with my sister Christine. We learnt how to play the bagpipes, the drums and the penny whistle.

When I was in my early twenties I was in a motorcycle accident, I was travelling to work on my Suzuki GN125 and was knocked off, as a result I had pins and plates in one of my legs and was very lucky not to lose my leg altogether. Although the majority of the metal work has been removed, I still have one broken screw remaining in my ankle which is still there to this day. In spite of this, I still enjoy swimming, going to the gym, and Zumba, here's a shout out to all the girls at Rhiannon's Parkrow Dance class. During the year that followed the bike accident I did a lot of writing and I think it was then that I decided at some point I'd like to write a novel.

This was not the first time a road accident changed my life. In November 1995 my sister Christine was killed in a road traffic accident, it was four days after her 15th birthday. The years that followed are a hazy fog of painful memories, confusion, denial, loss and heartbreak. Our family was shattered that night. Over the years we have all struggled to find our own way, I hope that life fares better for my children and that they never know grief like our family have experienced before they arrived. Life is unpredictable and one never knows what is around the corner. In life there is no dress rehearsal, and sometimes you just have to take a chance and go for things. This is me taking that chance. Based on a conversation I had with my Dad, Vengeance was created. I hope the reader enjoys, and if not that they are kind with constructive criticism as I am willing to hear feedback, as I will write again, although which direction that takes will depend on how this book goes.

Here's to taking chances in life, and seeing what the future holds.

All the best,

Tracy x